I0822451

The Crimson Rise

The Adventures of Junath Symp

N. D. Greenman

The Crimson Rise

The Adventures of Junath Symp

Illustrated by Lilly Suggs

The Crimson Rise: The Adventures of Junath Symp

Brickfielder™ is division and trademark of
Tole Publishing LLC™, Morgantown, KY 42261.

This book is a work of fiction. References to real events, organizations, or places are used in a fictional context. Any resemblances to actual persons, living or dead, are entirely coincidental.

ISBNS: 978-1-948696-61-6 (Paperback), 978-1-948696-64-7 (Hardback),
978-1-948696-63-0 (Kindle)

Library of Congress Control Number: 2023911679

Cover credits: owl silhouette © jan stopka; Junath with Lady, Midjourney (back cover for hardback only); all other images and graphics are under copyright and licensed through Canva
Interior credits: map © N. D. Greenman; all other illustrations © Lilly Suggs

Printed in the United States of America

TOLE PUBLISHING LLC, PO BOX 1098, MORGANTOWN, KY 42261-8411
www.brickfielderpub.com

Dedication:

To my grandmothers Elsie Barnes Phipps and Brenda Greenman. Two women who have inspired me to write, but first and foremost, to love and trust in the Lord.

Contents

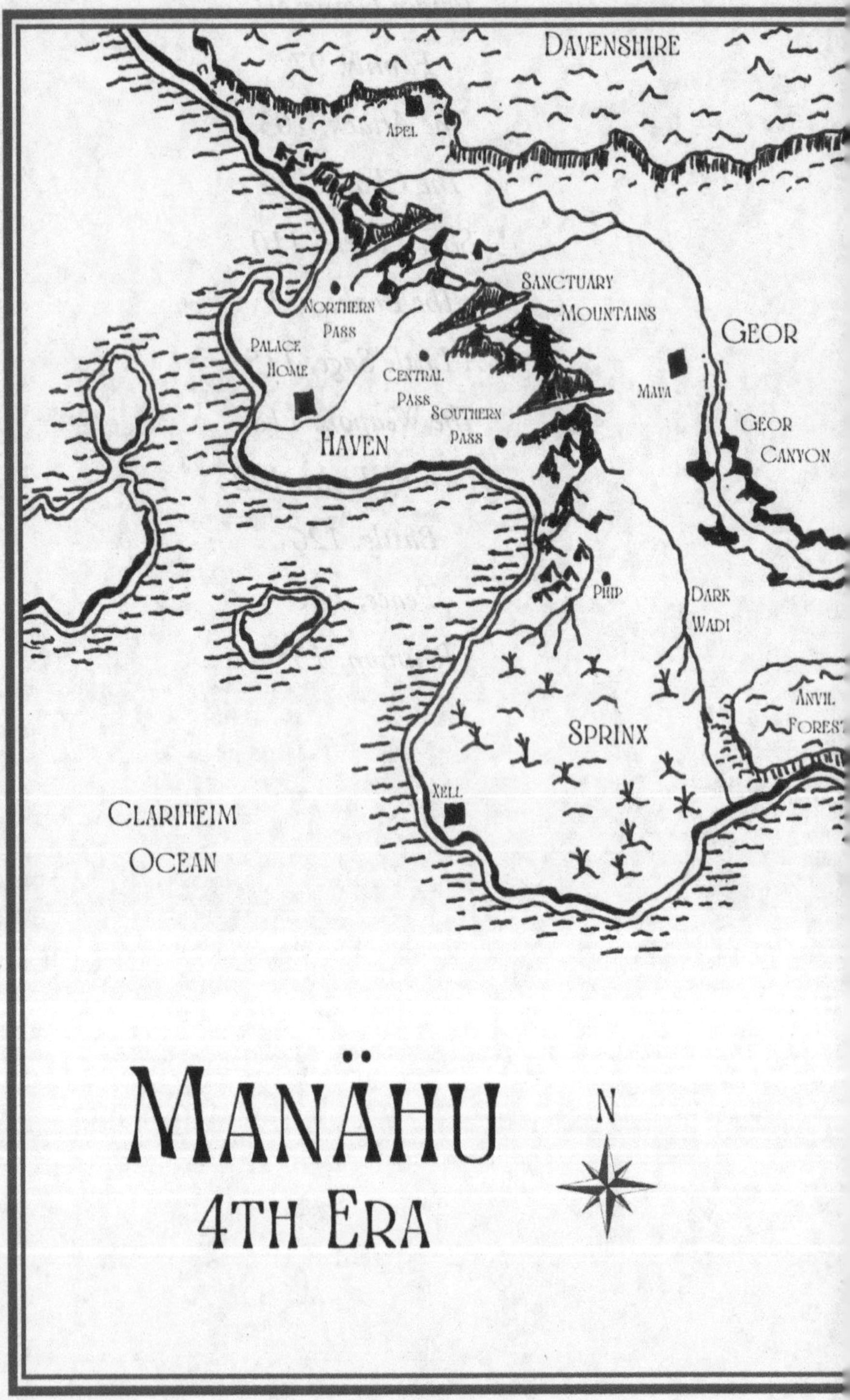

Davenshire
Apel
Sanctuary
Mountains
Geor
Northern
Pass
Palace
Home
Central
Pass
Southern
Pass
Mava
Haven
Geor
Canyon
Phip
Dark
Wadi
Anvil
Forest
Sprinx
Xell
Clariheim
Ocean

Manähu
4th Era

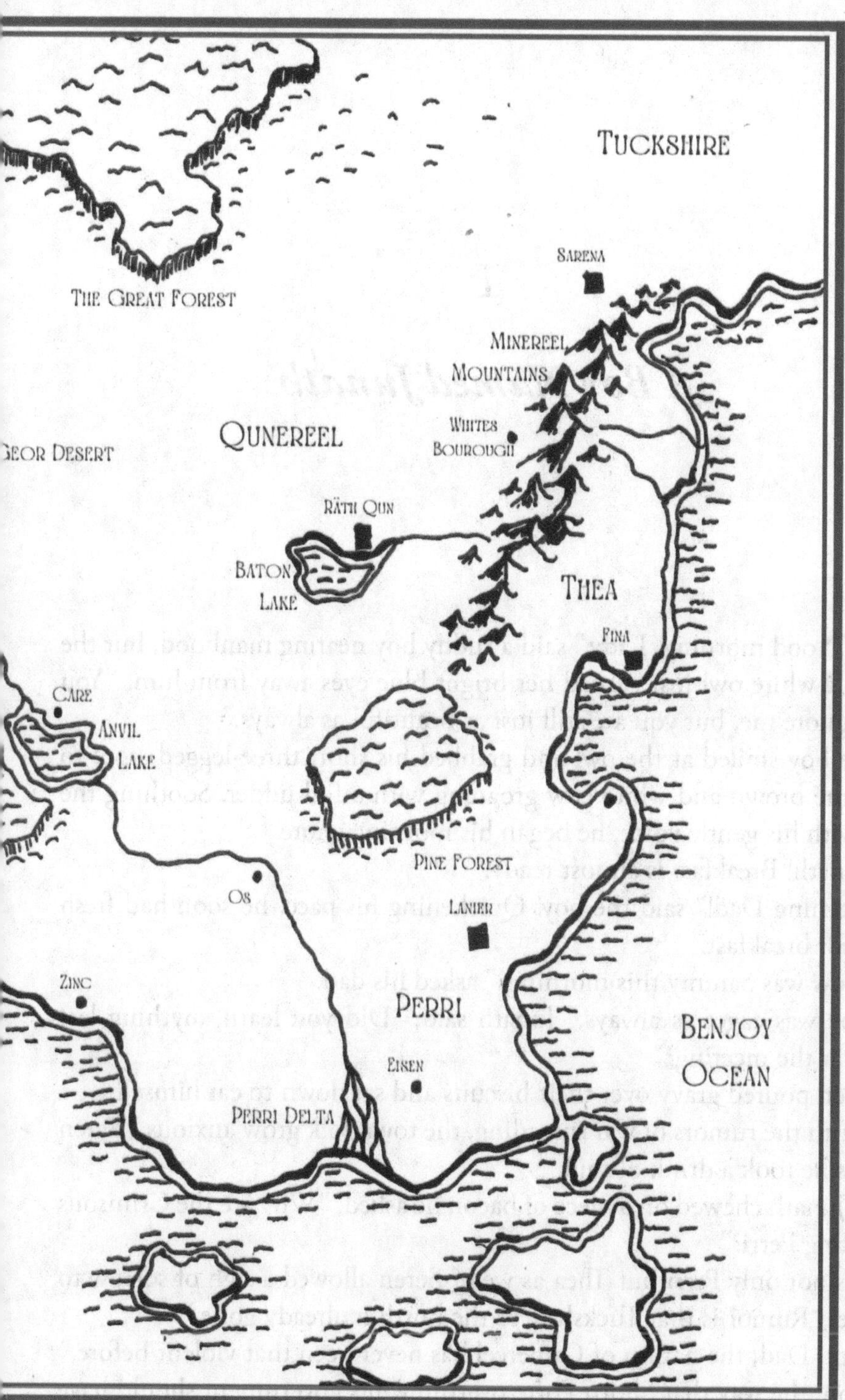

Tuckshire
The Great Forest
Sarena
Minereel
Mountains
Whites
Bourough
Qunereel
Geor Desert
Räth Qun
Baton
Lake
Thea
Fina
Care
Anvil
Lake
Pine Forest
Os
Lanier
Zinc
Perri
Benjoy
Ocean
Eisen
Perri Delta

I

A Boy Named Junath

"Good morning, Lady," said a ruddy boy nearing manhood, but the white owl just turned her bright blue eyes away from him. "You may ignore me, but you are still just as beautiful as always."

The boy smiled at the owl and grabbed his short three-legged stool to milk the brown and white cow groaning with a full udder. Soothing the cow with his gentle voice, he began his morning chore.

"Junath! Breakfast is almost ready!"

"Coming Dad!" said the boy. Quickening his pace, he soon had fresh milk for breakfast.

"How was Sammy this morning?" asked his dad.

"She was eager as always," Junath said, "Did you learn anything last night at the meeting?"

Seren poured gravy over their biscuits and sat down to eat himself.

"With the rumors of war spreading, the town folk grow anxious," Seren said as he took a drink of milk.

As Junath chewed on a piece of bacon he asked, "Why are the Crimsons attacking Perri?"

"It's not only Perri but Thea as well." Seren allowed a sigh of sorrow to escape. "Rumor is that Tuckshire to the north is already gone."

"But, Dad, the nation of Qunereel has never been that violent before."

"Son, the way that Shorn Forte overthrew his government should have told everyone that he was a cold, bloodthirsty soul."

Junath asked, "Is it true that Sprinx and Davenshire have given him their loyalty?"

"That's what I hear, and since Geor is undecided, it seems that Thea, Perri, and Haven are the only ones willing to stand up to him. In fact, Junny, the elders of Eisen are meeting this evening after dinner to discuss further reports received from Lanier and Fina."

"This is the fourth day in a row. We're going to be busy trying to get everything done and dinner ready before you leave."

Junath laid his fork down onto the plate with half of his breakfast still left. After a moment he asked, "Why does war have to come here?"

Seren, trying to comfort him, said, "A fifteen-year-old boy does not need to worry himself over something he cannot change. Strife comes and goes, and Ol' Forte will come to an end eventually. No one person can conquer all of Manähu. Besides, we poor farmers of the Perri Delta still have a farm to tend, and the corn's not going to pick itself."

Though uneasiness in the pit of his stomach continued, Junath genuinely smiled and replied, "Dad, you're right, worrying about the crops never causes them to grow any faster, and worrying about war won't keep it away. And today, it's not here."

"That's my boy, wise beyond his years, just like Jael. You two must get it from your mother. Come, let's go get that corn."

The two spent the morning harvesting some crops, but Seren needed to head back to the house and repair parts of the roof. Junath collected several bushels of corn for the crib and set some in the wagon for Seren to take to town that evening. Later in the afternoon, Seren allowed Junath to forego a couple of the less necessary chores so they could eat dinner early before he left.

At dinner, as Seren carved the chicken, he looked at Junath who was still pensive, quiet, and a little sullen. "Junath, the Crimson army is far away, and I told you that you don't need to worry about their lust for war."

"Dad, it's not the Crimsons, it's Jael."

Upon this revelation, Seren gently said, "Oh, I see."

Junath poured some water into their glasses, and Seren continued, "Jael left because he thought it best after your mother died. He figured he could work in the mines of Qunereel and maybe send some money back home."

Junath angrily replied, "But he has left us to rot, forcing you to raise me, run a farm, and now there is a threat of war…Jael's probably serving Shorn Forte as we speak!"

With a calm, authoritative voice, Seren corrected Junath, "I will not have you insult your brother in my presence again. He has chosen his path, and it has led him well. I assure you, Jael would not support the Crimson's lust for blood. He's not that kind of person. He has too much of his mother in him." After a pause, he added, "Don't doubt his love for us, it is stronger than you realize."

Junath, desiring not to rouse his father further, conceded the debate and moved on to more pleasant conversation.

After supper, Seren helped clean and then readied himself for the meeting. He hugged Junath and told him not to stay up waiting for his return. It would be late, and Junath needed to rise early to get a head start on his chores.

As Seren left, Junath began to complete his evening chores. Within a couple of hours, Junath finished and went and cleaned himself up to get ready for bed. He sat in Seren's rocking chair, and his thoughts continued to contemplate the war, Qunereel, and Jael. As he sat there watching the flames of the fire flicker, he became drowsy, and sleep was quickly upon him. Then he stood and threw a couple of split logs onto the fire to fight the chill of the night, and finally, he climbed into bed, drew his mother's patchwork quilt over him, and was soon fast asleep.

SLAM!

Junath jolted awake and found his father dashing madly through the house. Without even knowing why, Junath could taste the bile of vomit in his mouth.

2

Seren's Love

"Get dressed and pack your things like one of our hunting trips, but do it quickly!"

Without question, Junath began packing his hunting gear, a bow, a quiver of arrows, a skinning knife, and some rope. He also packed a couple of changes of clothes, eating utensils, and some food from the pantry. After he collected everything, he went to the front and began lacing his boots. Junath could hear Seren in a tumult in his bedroom. Junath grew more anxious.

"Dad, I am almost ready can you please tell…," Junath lost his voice when he looked up and saw Seren coming out of his room, ready for battle. Seren looked at Junath and finished strapping the family sword onto his waist. He wore leather armor, with bracers, greaves, boots, and a breastplate engraved with the royal seal of Perri. Junath had never seen this armor before, but he knew they were prized gifts from the king.

"Junath, let's get outside, and I will tell you what you need to know."

Outside, Seren looked to the northeast as if he were trying to see something, but Junath could see nothing. Seren turned to Junath and said very clearly, "You have to run. It is not safe here; you cannot stay. Now listen very closely because our time is short. You must make for Haven as quickly as possible. Find Jael and give him this." Seren handed Junath a rolled parchment with the Royal Seals of Thea and Perri imprinted on the reddish wax holding the parchment closed. "Make sure Jael gets this parchment, Junath. The fate of this war depends on it."

Because of the haste, the parchment, and the quest to find Jael in Haven, confusion began to swirl in Junath's head. He was coming up with far more questions than the answers Seren was giving.

"Dad, what's going on!"

As Seren handed him a tattered paper, he replied, "My dear boy, we are wanted men."

Junath looked at the paper and saw that two men were wanted by the Crimson Army. The two were Seren and Junath Symp, and under their pictures was the promise of a sum of money that would make a man set for years in the Perri Delta.

"What is this? We didn't do anything, did we Dad?"

"No, we haven't done anything. But because of this, you have to get to safety, and deliver this parchment to your brother." Seren looked down at Junath and saw Junath no longer as a child, but a boy thrust into manhood. Seren's eyes began to swell with tears knowing what must come next.

"Junath, I have been saving this, now you will need it." Seren handed Junath a heavy leather pouch that rang with the sound of coin. "Mr. Finson at the General Store wanted you to take his short sword for your journey. The town gives you their blessing."

While he strapped on Mr. Finson's short sword, Junath could hear horses in full gallop coming from the direction of town. A man could be heard giving orders, though the distance was too far to hear what was said.

"So Charlen and Mara have done all they could," said Seren in a whisper, though loud enough that Junath could hear it.

"What have Mr. and Mrs. Finson done?"

With a sigh, he said, "They kept the Crimsons occupied long enough to allow me to get home and let you escape, but it seems that the soldiers figured the truth." Seren then looked down at Junath and stared into his brown eyes. Junath was no longer just concerned, but terrified, and Seren could see it clearly on his son's face.

"Junath," Seren placed both hands on Junath's shoulders and softly said, "Much I have failed to say and now the time does not permit to do so. I know you are scared and confused, and you have every right to be, but you must trust me and rush to Haven to find Jael. Now run, don't turn back, and don't stop until daylight to rest." Seren pointed west, and when he gave a final command to run, he pushed Junath in the direction he should go. Junath did not hesitate, but obeyed his father and ran into the grove of palm trees that indicated the edge of his farm and the beginning of the delta rivers. A couple of rows of trees in, Junath stopped and turned to see his father, hoping he was right behind him. But what Junath saw was far from that hope.

With a drawn sword, Seren faced the oncoming cavalry unit. Though it was night, the moonlight held nothing back, and with skill and precision, they guided their horses to surround Seren. Their horses were all the same color brown, and the Crimson uniform was solid black except for an embroidered patch on the right shoulder. It was difficult to tell, but Junath thought it depicted a crimson ribbon wound around a silver sword, and beginning at the top of their left shoulder a braided cord of the same crimson color looped itself around the soldier's arm.

When the dust began to settle, the commander of the cavalry unit looked down at Seren and commanded, "Seren Symp, I place you under arrest by the authority of Shorn Forte, Supreme Commander of the Crimson Forces and the King of Qunereel. You are also ordered to surrender Junath Symp. To resist will result in your death."

Seren stared deep into the commander's eyes. He did not hesitate or lower his sword but solemnly replied, "Shorn Forte is a tyrant and a bloodthirsty fool. He only wants what he can't have, and neither me nor Junath had anything to do with his Isabella."

"Mr. Symp, let me remind you that to resist will cost you your life. And anymore slandering of our General and King will cause you to suffer greatly while in captivity." The commander looked coldly at Seren, and it was evident that his threat contained no bluff.

But Seren continued, "Forte is a loose cannon, and he will be the death of us all before this war is finished. But tonight, he will not have the joy or satisfaction to hold me and my son captive. Junath is already gone, and you will never catch him."

The commander sighed and finally said, "Mr. Symp, you are a foolish old man, and your boy will be caught before the sun rises."

"As long as I have breath and life in my arms, Junath gets further out of your reach."

Through his snarling lips, the commander replied, "So be it, arrest the old man, and if he resists, strike him dead where he stands." A couple of soldiers dismounted to arrest Seren, but to their surprise, the "old man" was not about to go quietly in the night.

Seren effortlessly disarmed the two soldiers who approached him and tripped the first and knocked out the second with the hilt of his sword. Three more soldiers quickly dismounted and more cautiously approached Seren with readied blades, but they too proved to be light work for Seren's skill.

Junath watched with amazement and awe at the swordsmanship displayed by his father. Though he heard many rumors of Seren's ability while in town, he never really believed them because he never saw Seren fight or practice with his blade. Each time he would question his father on the matter, Seren would casually chuckle and say, "My boy, some people exaggerate when a man survives the battles of his youth. I was just a lucky man." Now Junath saw the skill he possessed.

Ten soldiers now surrounded Seren and were far more calculated in their approach. Seren twirled and twisted, parried and blocked, and then he sidestepped to evade their crushing blows while incapacitating another soldier. Four more men lay at his feet when a black dart from a crossbow entered Seren's shoulder.

The commander started reloading. Seren, in excruciating pain, still warded off the approaching men. Another dart flew into Seren's side. Seren tried to parry another blow, but the dart prevented him. His opponent's sword came sliding across his calf muscle. Seren dropped to his knees. A third arrow pierced his armor. Clutching the final bolt, Seren Symp collapsed silently onto the ground.

3

Junath's Peril

"No!" The words left Junath's mouth before he realized his mistake. The Crimson commander immediately picked up on Junath's location and ordered his men to pursue him. As the soldiers remounted their horses, they charged into the grove of trees. Junath bolted deeper into the Perri Delta.

The commander could be heard barking, "Don't return unless you have that boy!" and "I'll have your head if you return empty!" A fire burned in the eyes of the commander as he witnessed Junath elude the horsemen.

Under his breath, the commander whispered, "Those idiots will lose that boy," and then he yelled, "Corporal Johnson, return to me!" When the young corporal returned, he was ordered to take Seren's lifeless body back to camp. The commander charged into the delta to ensure that the mission was successful.

Though the delta had trees, the landscape was mainly bushes, waterways, and flat strips of land which allowed the horsemen to keep an eye on Junath, but Junath corralled the hunting pack into rivers or deep mud, ensnaring their horses. A couple of times, clouds would cover the moon, and he would utilize the quick darkness to hide behind a bush or two, but it only served to confuse the soldiers temporarily.

The commander, on the other hand, decided to run ahead and flank Junath. He could see the general direction Junath was taking and saw the traps which his men were finding themselves. He charged his horse upstream, and after a few hundred yards, he found a shallow crossing. He looked south to see the direction of his prey, and then he drove his horse west, outrunning his men and Junath.

He turned south to intercept Junath and found a perfect spot for an ambush. The commander prepared his crossbow.

Entirely focused on ridding himself of the last horsemen, Junath was oblivious to the commander ahead of him. Junath began climbing the little knoll, and the moment he topped the ledge, he heard a cold chuckle. Panting for breath, Junath dropped to his knees. He had been beaten.

"How unfortunate that you must die," said the commander. "You have great potential, but to strike you down will serve me so much more. That pathetic Jael will break and crumble. He was always the sentimental type. What a worthless man."

"What do you know about my brother?" said Junath with defiant spirit.

"I know much of that coward, and I will treasure the day I can tell him that both his father and brother are dead," the commander lifted his crossbow and continued, "Now, tell me everything you know and I will allow your death to be swift."

The last horseman finally reached the top of the knoll and guided his horse to tower over Junath. Junath looked at his hands clutching the parchment, and then the death of his father replayed in his thoughts. With sharp fiery eyes, Junath looked up at the commander and said, "Mister, I don't know what this parchment is all about, or why you boorish louts want me, but I know that you murdered my father and I will be a dead man before you ever get this or anything else from me."

The commander aimed, and said, "That, my boy, can be arranged."

Just as the commander pulled the trigger, a white flash came from behind Junath, which was quickly followed by a gust of wind. Junath felt no pain, but the horseman beside Junath didn't fare as well, and he fell with the arrow in his chest. Junath looked up at the commander who was in the middle of a brilliant battle with a large white bird. He began wailing, screaming, and was desperately fighting the bird off his face.

Junath hesitated only a second, and he took advantage of this remarkable change of events. As he ran away into the dark, he turned and saw the commander clutching his face. The bird had flown off.

Junath watched the commander ball up his fists and belt out a shrill scream and yell, "Junath Symp, Run away! Run away! But I swear I will hunt you down and murder you myself. You hear me?! I, Finister Kein, will kill you before you get within a hundred leagues of Haven." Finister Kein continued to yell more threats and curses, but Junath began his journey and was soon out of earshot of those who wanted him dead.

Junath did not stop but to take short breaks and drink some water. After a few hours of running, he found himself halfway through the delta. The moon was lowering, and Junath was exhausted. He decided to camp for the night. He crawled under a bush, put his pack under his head, and the thoughts of his father's sacrifice plagued his restless mind. Finally consumed with grief, the young man cried. Then he slept.

4

Lady

It was nearing midday and Junath was still sleeping. Suddenly, someone began to tap on his arm. Junath jolted awake ready to fight when he realized that the one doing the tapping was none other than Lady, the owl that took residence in his barn.

Confusion swirled within Junath's head and then he remembered his flight from home the night before and recalled how a large bird attacked Finister Kein allowing Junath to escape. He looked upon Lady and figured that she was his savior.

"Thank you, Lady," said Junath softly. He stared into her large blue eyes and admired her beauty. No other bird could match her prowess, grace, and ability. He reached his hand out to touch her and she gently leaned in for the pet. She was covered in white feathers, but black feathers speckled through her plumage. She was soft and soothing to the touch.

She twisted her head to look around and let out a soft "hoo." A rabbit hopped out from behind another bush twenty yards away. Lady stretched out her wings. Junath figured her wingspan had to be nearly as long as he was tall. With one great beat with her wings, she was several feet in the air. He watched her climb and make a large circle. She bent her wings just slightly and dove for the ground. Had the rabbit known that a great hunter of the night was making her approach, he probably would have scurried back into his hole, but he did not. Silently, Lady flew in and clasped the rabbit in her talons, and within a blink of the eye, she was back in the air.

Lady arched toward Junath and landed where she had taken off just moments ago. She released the rabbit and Junath saw that the prize was for him. He smiled and with a slight chuckle said, "Lady, you sure are a sight for sore eyes. Not only do you save my life, but you also bring me breakfast in bed."

Junath saw that the rabbit was still alive, and he reached for his hunting knife and put the poor creature out of his misery. Junath enjoyed hunting, and he definitely valued what a hunted animal could provide for sustenance and for tools, but he never relished having to put creatures to death. It was a sad but needed process in the world. So, he put the animals to rest as quickly and painlessly as possible.

With the sun high and bright, Junath decided that he could light a fire and not be seen. He made sure that he used extremely dry wood so as not to create any smoke. He cleaned the rabbit and gave a portion to Lady as compensation for her labor and then he roasted the rabbit over the small fire until it was thoroughly cooked. After running all night and the stress of the events of the night before, Junath realized he was famished and devoured the tender meat.

Junath decided to sit and rest for a few moments and then continued on his journey. Somehow, he had to make his way to Haven. Though he was somewhat familiar with the geography of Manähu, he knew that he did not really know the way. After thinking for a few minutes, he spoke out loud, "If I keep west I will run into a road leading to Zinc, and perhaps I can hire someone to be my guide."

He had been to Zinc once in his life with Seren. They went there to celebrate the Festival of Harvests. Each year a different city in Perri hosted the festival. Four years ago Zinc was the host. Though Seren was not much of a traveler, he felt it would be enlightening and a joyful respite for Junath to see more of his country.

Junath stared into the west and said, "Lady, I must be off. I am being hunted and I must stay ahead of those who want me dead." He rolled up his blanket, gathered his things, and set off hiking through the delta. Lady kept a close eye on Junath and flew within close proximity of him. Junath noticed how she stayed with him and it brought him comfort.

Mysteries of the night burdened Junath, and the questions he had were not going to soon be answered. Why were he and his father wanted?

Wanted by the Crimsons even! Yet as hard as he thought, Junath had no answers to his questions.

Junath hiked for several hours and the sun was beginning to set in the west. He took a break and refilled his water skin. He did not want to risk a fire so close to night, so he reached into his pack, pulled out some jerky and a piece of bread. A meager dinner, but one that would keep him content for several hours. Lady flew off to hunt while he chewed the tough meat.

Within a few minutes Lady returned, seemingly satisfied after a successful hunt. Junath continued to stare off into the west and then said to the owl, "By morning we should reach the edge of the Delta, I figure the Crimsons will be patrolling the western edge, waiting for me to walk into their arms. I do believe it will be best to travel by night for a little while."

As the grey of dawn began to appear, he spotted the edge of the delta. He settled down under the cover of a few bushes and allowed sleep to take his body. He rested quite soundly. A few times throughout the day he would hear suspicious sounds which would cause him to wake, but they only proved to be small vermin or the wind.

After his rest was over, Junath rose and had another meal of jerky, bread, and water. He did not dare test his fortune by lighting a fire so close to the edge. As the sun began to set and dusk was nigh upon them, Junath began the final leg through the Perri Delta. Lady flew on ahead.

About an hour into the hike, Junath reached the edge. He crawled and listened for any sentries searching the area and sure enough he spotted three on horseback heading in his direction. Fear gripped Junath. A small grove of trees lay twenty yards northwest. If he could reach the grove, he figured he could hideout and remain concealed, but the grove was in the direction of the horsemen.

A small window, if any, existed and if he was to take advantage of it, the time was now. Junath's hesitation lost him the opportunity. By the time he decided to risk it, the soldiers on horseback were too close. They were so close he could even make out their conversation.

"I'm sick of this pathetic search for some boy." The man's voice was immature and sounded rather obnoxious. Junath figured he was a young recruit.

The second voice Junath heard was deep, rich, and obviously annoyed. He was saying, "Quiet, Sandson, we must keep an ear out for him, and he is not some pathetic boy, or General Forte would not be wanting him or offering such a reward."

Then the third voice, somewhere between a baritone and tenor, spoke, "I personally would prefer to spend my time fighting the Perrian army, earning my honor and fame through battle, not chasing some farm boy across some forsaken land."

"You'll get your time, I'm sure of that, but our orders are to find this boy, and the sooner we do, the sooner we can put this patrol behind us," said the second voice. The other two men agreed.

Fearing capture, Junath grew restless. He slid his sword out silently and readied it for an attack. He whispered to Lady, "I guess we will have to fight our way out of this one too."

Lady, on the other hand, tucked her wings up tight and squatted closer to the ground and looked up. Junath followed her gaze and saw a wonder he had believed to be only fiction. A vessel that was able to defy gravity and fly through the air as a ship does in the water.

5

A Man of Mystery

Though the shadow of night prevented Junath from making out any particulars of the airship, he could hear the creaking of wood as the ship flapped wings like oars. Even as a silhouette, it still left him queasy. Yet, his curiosity desired to see the ship in daylight so he could inspect it in detail. Machinery had always interested him. His brother Jael, while on the farm, invented a countless number of mechanized machines to help facilitate the work. It was the one thing he still appreciated about this brother.

Junath sat there frozen and almost forgot that the sentries were nearly upon him. He came to his senses, gripped his sword, and renewed his resolve to fight the soldiers regardless of what would come from the airship. Then at the point when Junath feared the sentries would spot him, a horn blasted from the airship, signaling its arrival.

"General Kein must want an update," said the second soldier. "Come on, let's go see what he wants. Maybe he found this boy." The three horsemen turned the horses around and quickened the their pace to a steady gallop. Junath did not waste his new opportunity, and he ran for the trees.

He made it with no indication that he was seen by the sentries or the airship. Lady was near, flying above. Junath ran and increased the distance between him and the soldiers. The forest began to grow thicker, making it more challenging to progress. By the first light of morning, Junath had grown weary and found shelter under some brush and a fallen log to rest.

A few hours had passed when the rustling of an animal awakened Junath. Thinking it was Lady, Junath said, "You have a good catch today?" But to Junath's horror, it was not Lady, and through the thicket, he saw a large white wolf. At the sound of his voice, the wolf turned her attention toward his sound. It did not take the wolf long, and she spotted Junath under the log. She began to walk toward Junath as if stalking easy prey. In his haste, Junath decided to make a run for it trying to find a tree to climb.

The wolf effortlessly chased Junath through the woods, and then Junath spotted the perfect tree to make a quick escape. As he was just two strides from reaching the tree, he tripped over a root, and he plummeted to the ground. He scrambled to his feet, reached for his sword, and faced his enemy. With adrenaline pumping and boiling anger from the fall, Junath's voice cracked, "Come on wolf! I won't be taken that easy!"

But she was mindful and sauntered around Junath, waiting for the right moment to strike. For several moments she waited patiently, then with a growl, she rushed toward Junath.

"Iris, heel!" A strong voice sounded through the forest, and with a quick jerk, the wolf ran toward the voice. Junath could see no one, and he searched for any sign of the man who called the wolf away.

The man spoke again, "You best not be Crimson, or I'll let Iris use your sword to pick your bones from her teeth."

Junath replied, "I…I am not Crimson, and who is it that speaks to me with threatening words?"

"I am one you do not want to cross, and I'll be the judge whether you are Crimson or not." As he finished speaking, a hooded figure with a ready longbow stepped out from behind a tree. The concealed man began walking toward Junath, and Junath began to grow anxious. He then noticed Lady was high in the tree observing the exchange, and the fact that she did not seem too concerned relieved some of the tension in Junath's muscles.

Junath looked to the man and said, "I have no quarrel with you. I only desire to head west in peace."

"Too late for that. Occasionally, I am a curious type, and besides, if you are Crimson, I would rather see you dead." As the man approached, Junath realized how futile it was to keep his sword out, and hoping it would demonstrate his desire for peace, he placed the sword into its sheath.

"That's a foolish thing to do," said the man.

Junath replied, "What's the use? Your arrow would pierce me long before I took two steps toward you with my sword. I was hoping that it showed that I desire no quarrel with you."

"Iris come!" At the command of the man, the wolf reappeared and trotted up to her master. "Watch him. If he makes a sudden move, attack him."

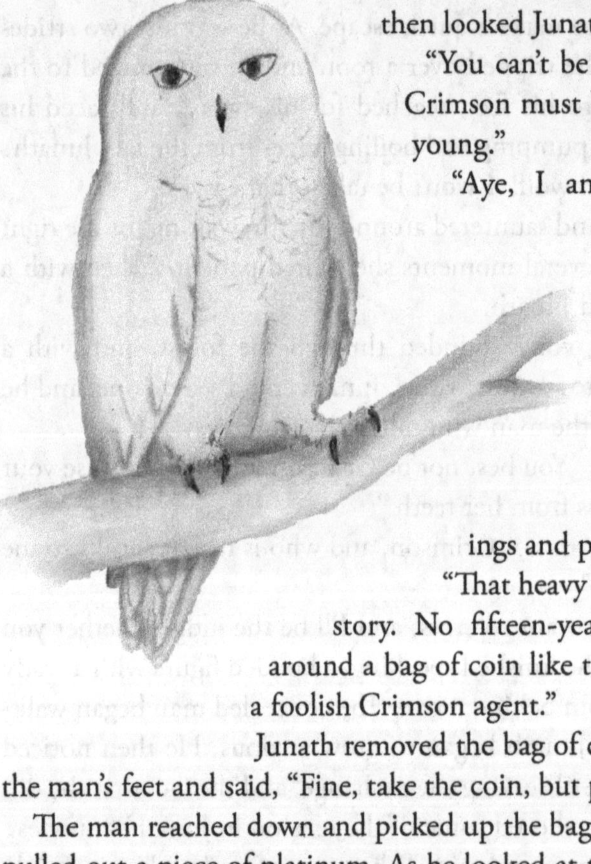

The man then lowered his bow and allowed it to relax, but he kept the arrow strung. He then looked Junath over.

"You can't be much over fifteen. The Crimson must be desperate to enlist so young."

"Aye, I am fifteen, but I'm no Crimson." Junath was beginning to get a little angry with the Crimson accusations.

"Well, what is in your bag?"

"Just my belongings and personal things."

"That heavy money bag tells another story. No fifteen-year-old vagabond carries around a bag of coin like that unless he's a thief or a foolish Crimson agent."

Junath removed the bag of coins and threw them at the man's feet and said, "Fine, take the coin, but please let me be."

The man reached down and picked up the bag and opened it. He then pulled out a piece of platinum. As he looked at the inscription, the man said in slightly above a whisper, "Well, this changes things." Looking to Junath, he asked, "Who gave you this money?"

"My father did."

"Who is your father?"

"That's a private matter."

"I certainly would like to know who he is." The man threw the bag of coins back. "The coins are from Haven, and no Crimson in his right mind would be caught carrying anything from there."

Puzzeled at the revelation, Junath whispered, "Haven?"

The man removed his hood. The man's hair was iron grey and cropped close. He wore a short stubble beard with white patches on his jaw near his chin. He was thin but well built. His eyes were blue and as clear as fresh rainwater, and his face had defined lines, but not the wrinkles of an elderly man.

"My name is Cal Whist, Iris and I are travelers too. You seem to be far from home, but you don't seem to be from Haven."

Junath carefully replied, "Haven isn't my home; it's where I'm going. If you don't mind, I would like to keep my name and history to myself. I have been called Nate by friends in the past, and that should be sufficient for a name for now."

"Hmm, very well…Nate… I expect you're hungry, and since I have caused you a great ordeal, at least let me provide you with some breakfast."

6

A Hero Lost

The conversation during breakfast was rather simple and neither Junath nor Cal volunteered a lot of information. Sitting by the fire, Junath sat and stared at nothing, but was lost in his thoughts, filled with sorrow, hatred, bitterness, and on the brink of despair.

Cal tapped Junath on the shoulder to shake him out of his stupor and asked, "Who did you lose?"

"Who said I lost anyone?"

"Son, I have seen death more times than I ever care to see again. I know the look one has when he has lost someone close."

"My dad. He died several nights ago. Some Crimson soldiers killed him."

"Ahh…I see. I am sorry…"

Saying it out loud caused Junath to lose his control and he began to weep. When he finally calmed down, looking at the ground he said, "He died saving my life! I should have fought and died alongside him, but I was a coward. I was a coward!" Junath slumped and continued to weep.

"Listen, you are right to be angry, but don't blame yourself. Your father did what he thought best. I too would have wanted my son free. I too would rather be dead instead of my son. He sacrificed his life, so you could have yours. Grieve for your loss, yes, but don't beat yourself up because of it. Make it to Haven fulfilling the wishes of a dying man."

Junath did not reply, but his sobbing eased. He stood and took a couple of steps west and stared through the trees as if trying to see something in the distance that was not there. He raised his hand and placed it upon a birch tree rubbing the rough bark under his palm. Quietly, Junath spoke, "He sacrificed himself so the Crimson wouldn't get both of us. I don't understand…I just don't get why they came after my father and me. We were just two poor farmers living to make it through each day. Why?"

Cal looked at him and meditated upon who the young man was that stood before him. He recalled hearing rumors of a father and son who were wanted by the Crimsons. He recalled the father's name from the Wars against the Seabearers nearly thirty years ago. Though Cal fought in the wars too, he never met Seren but heard well of his deeds. He remembered the rewards were hefty for Seren and his son, Junath, but no one knew why. Cal thought to himself, "Surely this isn't Seren's son before my eyes. If this boy is Junath, then the great Seren Symp must be dead."

As Cal continued to think, he decided to ask again the young boy his identity. He stood and walked over to Junath and examined his face. He had seen drawings of Seren in the chronicles of the Wars. He had little doubt now. "Are you Junath, the son of Seren? "

Junath, horror on his face, replied, "How…Aye, I am he."

Then Cal solemnly said, "Then the hero and defender of Manähu is dead."

7

A Party of Four

If the mysteries surrounding this plight to Haven to find Jael were not enough to perplex Junath, the new twist that Cal not only knew who he and his father were but that this stranger knew the deeds of his father completely mystified him.

As Junath stared at the man who identified him, he asked, "Mister, I give you the credit for figuring out who I am. You probably remember seeing me on some wanted poster, but I must ask you something and perhaps, you can solve one of the mysteries revealed since the night my father died. What did you mean when you said, 'Then the hero and defender of Manähu is dead?'"

Cal, not sure what Junath was reaching for, simply replied, "I meant what I said, your father, Seren, was a great man of valor against our foe the Seabearers some thirty years ago. Certainly, you know who your father was?"

"I fear I don't know anything anymore…That night when he died, I saw things from him that I never knew the slightest detail about. Sure I heard rumors in town, but he always denied them or brushed them off as some adventure of a foolish youth. His armor that he wore that night had the king's mark, and it was obviously very valuable, the kind that is gifted by the king himself. And Oh, how he fought…I have heard of men with that swordsmanship but only from the story-tellers." Junath stared at the ground as he recalled that fateful night.

Cal placed his hand on Junath's shoulder and said, "I am sorry your father has died, and that you were made to witness it. Strange that he would keep his past a secret, but men do what they deem best. I am sure he had a good reason why he did what he did. He was indeed a great man. Though I never knew him personally, I certainly heard of his feats in the war. He was a strong and virtuous man, one who fought as a sacrifice for the lives of his people. The way he died for you accentuates the strong moral fiber that knit him together."

Junath looked up at Cal, thankful that he had found someone who did not seem to be an enemy. He remained quiet as he chewed on the words that Cal spoke, and then after a few minutes, he rose and went to his pack. He pulled out the bag of coins and the sealed parchment. As he walked over to Cal, he said, "That entire night is shrouded in mystery. He charged me to deliver this parchment to my brother in Haven. My brother deserted us when I was three years old and I have never seen or heard from him since. He left for Qunereel to work in the mines to 'send money' back to us. Funny that I should find him all the way out west. But I still ask myself, 'Why my brother, and why does this parchment have the royal seal? Why did my father have it? Why did my father have a huge bag of coins from Haven?' Cal, I fear my father kept more from me than just his personal history."

"Questions will be answered in their time, but if that parchment has the royal seal, then it is imperative that it reaches its intended audience. I have you know, you are not the only person confused or concerned why you and your father were sought after by the Crimsons. It is a huge source of gossip amongst those for and against the conquest of the Crimsons. Many hoped it was a sign your father was rising to the occasion to lead the people against Shorn Forte and his Crimson Army, but alas, that hope is dead." Cal grabbed Junath by the shoulders and looked into his eyes and said, "But a new mission is afoot and knowing that the Crimsons are desperately looking for you, I have half a mind to help you to Haven. What do you say? Fancy having a lonely old man and his wolf join your party?"

Though Junath knew his answer, he had a particular request first, "Will you teach me your skill as a ranger?"

"Young man, of course I will."

With little delay, they packed up and began their trek west in search of Junath's brother in the land of Haven.

8

A Tracker Is Born

Cal knelt down, studying the ground. Junath leaned over trying to look at what Cal was seeing. Cal circled his hand around and said, "Our dinner is moving northwest. We're probably an hour behind him."

Junath looked at the grass and then back at Cal saying, "I see only grass."

"Yes, but what does the grass tell you?"

"Um, that it's green?"

Cal laughed, pointed at the grass, and said, "No, look, see how this grass is bent as if it's been stepped on?"

Junath squatted down looking and he did see the bent grass. It was a small area, but he could read it. "Yeah, I see it, but what does mean?"

"As a tracker, we learn to read the land like you read a scroll. Once you learn the words, then you can comprehend the message. You see, the grass is bent. It's just a small area, but this grass tells us many things. One, we are still going in the right direction from when we saw the fresh print in the mud thirty minutes ago, but also, grass restores after a couple of hours. The fact that we see this grass bent shows it hasn't been long since the print was made so we're getting closer. Nothing can walk through the meadow or woods without leaving a trail, no matter how agile and swift it may be. This is something we need to keep in mind since we are being tracked too."

Junath studied the grass, burning the image into his mind. Then taking a few steps farther up, he stooped down and examined the grass again, "Here, here's another." Junath was quite excited to actually see it.

"Good eye, and look up a bit farther, you see that? There's some droppings. If they are fresh, then this open meadow is its feeding spot. Let's check it out."

As they walked up to the next site, the animal droppings were indeed fresh. Cal said, "We can continue to follow this animal, and by the look of these droppings, we are following a deer of the same size as the one that made the tracks we saw. If we were to follow, we could run the risk of spooking it, and then we would be at square one. However, since this is a feeding spot, we could climb up one of those trees on the edge and wait for the deer to return."

The pair found a solid tree downwind of the meadow, climbed about halfway up and were able to get a good view of the deer's feeding ground. Lady perched herself in an upper branch, and Iris curled up under a bush while Cal and Junath waited for dinner.

About an hour later, a large buck gracefully paraded onto the meadow as if he was checking for danger. When he leaned down to eat, several more deer ventured out onto the meadow to graze. Junath whispered, "Are we going to take the large buck?" Cal placed a finger over his mouth to silence Junath, and then he pulled his bow back to full strength, aimed, and fired. In a moment the arrow flew under the deer's neck disappearing into the grass, the deer stampeded out of the meadow into the heart of the woods.

Junath, a little disappointed said, "You missed."

Cal's reply was, "So it seems. Come, let's retrieve the arrow."

As they approached the lost arrow, Cal told Junath where to find it. Junath walked up and saw the fletching. Reaching down to pick it up, it soon became evident to Junath that Cal didn't miss. As he lifted the arrow up, he saw it had pierced three hefty rabbits.

"Tracking the deer was for practice. We needed something lighter so we could move on quickly. These rabbits will serve us well for dinner and breakfast. Come, let me show you how to build a fire pit that is easily concealed."

Cal took Junath into the woods to help camouflage their camp. Choosing a tree and some brush to help conceal the firepit, Cal took his spade and dug a circle about two feet in diameter. Allowing the roots of the grass to maintain the sod, he lifted the patch up and set it off to the side saying, "When we break camp, we can reassemble this pit and most won't be any wiser we were here." He finished the hole to about a foot deep and then made a smaller hole in the direction of the wind. "This hole will burrow into the bigger pit to allow airflow, thus keeping our fire going." Pulling out some tinder he had collected back in the meadow, he struck a piece of flint he had to start the flame. Setting the burning tinder into the pit, he began to coax the fire into a hearty blaze, while it remained invisible to anyone who may have been looking for signs of a fire.

Junath, Cal, and Iris each ate a rabbit, while Lady enjoyed the rabbit organs. Cal looked up and said, "We have a few hours before the sun will set. Let's rest, and then we can continue our hike during the night. Iris will keep a look out for us." Both slept and once the sun was down and the camp was cleaned, the party of four set out.

9

Friendship Deepens

The following three weeks were quite uneventful. Cal led them northwest parallel to the Anvil River, but he was careful to keep a few miles west of the river, fearing that the Crimsons were always searching. Night travel was their preferred time of travel. During the day, they could keep a lookout for potential sentries and the airship. Apparently, Cal was well informed of the contraption that Junath had seen in the night sky.

During their three weeks of travel, Cal continued instructing Junath on the skills of a hunter and a ranger. Junath made substantial progress, but Cal reminded him that to master the trade, it would take years of diligent practice.

On the morning of the first day of the fourth week, Cal decided to enter the small city of Os. While finishing breakfast, Cal looked over to Junath and said, "Junath, I will go to the city and buy supplies. Os is a small town, but one that hears plenty of gossip. I will prod around and see if I can find out any more about you, and what news is available about the Crimsons during the past month. You remain here with Lady and Iris. I should return in two days' time."

"Is Haven's platinum and gold welcomed in town? I can give you some to buy the supplies you need." As Junath said these words, he began reaching for his purse.

"I fear we have no choice. We really need the supplies and hopefully, I will find someone who is not sympathetic to the Crimsons to deal with. It will be a gamble, but one that I have made more than once in the past."

Junath handed Cal the purse and told him to take what he needed. Cal removed three gold pieces and twenty silver pieces. He refused to use any platinum for that large a coin would most certainly raise some questions in such a small city. If he were in Care or Phip, he would certainly use that money, but not in Os.

As Cal tucked the money away, he looked at Junath and said, "While I am away, I want you to use Iris and Lady to practice your hunting and tracking skills. Command Iris to hide and she will. If you cannot find her, just call her name and she will return. Use Lady to help you see what you cannot."

"I will Cal, and be careful."

"You do what I said, and don't you worry about me. I've had my head on the chopping block before and managed to escape without a scratch. I'll be mindful, but if I am not back in a week, you must begin your journey on your own." Upon saying these words, Cal silently ran in the direction of the city of Os.

Junath began immediately with his studies. Lady's eyesight could detect the light path caused by Iris and would help guide Junath by looking in the direction of the track. But Iris was keen herself and knew her job well. Junath was able to search for her only a few times over the next couple of days. His best time was five hours. Learning how to use Lady as an aid and a partner developed rapidly.

By the end of the second day, Junath expected to see Cal, but his expectation went unfulfilled. When three more days passed without a word from Cal, he grew concerned. Looking to Iris and Lady he said, "I think we may need to head to Os too."

Iris whined and made a motion to go in the direction Cal had been leading them. "No, Iris," said Junath, "I don't think Cal would have abandoned us, and we can't abandon him. We must try something." She came over and rubbed her head against Junath and began a trek toward Os while Lady flew high and ahead.

10

Os

Cal made it to the gates around noon on the day he left. Crimson soldiers were everywhere. Cal's first place to stop was the message boards. Junath's picture was everywhere. Seren was removed. The reward for Junath's capture was substantially increased from the last time Cal had read the wanted notices. He muttered under his breath, "We're going to have to be extra careful..."

Cal decided his next stop would be the stables. The smell of hay and manure wafted in the air as Cal entered the wooden structure. Finding a man grooming one of the horses he approached and said, "I need two good riding horses."

Without turning to Cal but focusing on his brushing, the horse manager replied, "Good horses are hard to come by with the Crimson's buying them up. If I can track a couple down, they will be pricey."

"What's pricey?"

He paused his grooming and rubbed a stubbled chin. After a moment he answered, "Oh, with scoutin' them, testin' them, gearin' them up, I reckon the cost would supply me near a year."

"I'll give you 20 ounces of silver for each horse."

"I'll need at least two ounces of gold to make any profit."

"I have an ounce of gold and 10 ounces of silver." Cal looked into the merchant's eyes without blinking.

"One ounce of gold, plus the original 20 ounces of silver you offered, I will be happy to make the deal."

Cal considered the offer. The prices were not bad for two good horses, equipped and ready to ride, so he replied, "Fine, I'll take the deal, but I will only give you the silver until I am able to check the horses out myself. When you bring me the horses, I will give you the rest of the money."

"Fair enough. Give me till noon tomorrow and I will have your horses here at the stables."

Cal handed the money over, and the merchant looked at the coins and a slight scowl crossed his face, but it quickly vanished behind a smile, and he said, "Be careful, Ranger, and see you tomorrow."

Cal turned, uncomfortable about the look on the merchant's face, and he resolved to be very vigilant when he returned to get the horses. His next stop was the weapons and armor bazaar to buy Junath a battle bow, a full quiver, and some leather armor. The vendor proved to be patriotic to the resistance against the Crimsons, and when he saw the coin was from Haven, he cut Cal an even better deal. The same went for the vendor who sold salt and other seasonings for food.

By the end of the day, Cal had purchased all he felt he needed to buy. It was just a matter of waiting for the horses, and the uneasy feeling came over him again. Normally, Cal would instantly follow his intuition, but because he had to get Junath to Haven quickly, he ignored his gut feeling and planned to continue with caution.

The next day, Cal rose early and went to scout the area around the stables. The horse handler had two great looking horses saddled up and ready to go. Cal was starting to think that he was overreacting yesterday when a Crimson officer walked up to the handler.

Cal closed his eyes and turned his ear to hear their conversation. The officer said, "My men are in place, you sure this ranger is an agent of Haven?"

"Here is the money he gave me, and he was very secretive, unlike any I had seen before."

Cal exclaimed through his breath, "What a pig!" He decided to leave the city and find rides elsewhere, but guards were stationed at the gates. No doubt they were searching for him. Cal had to find another way out of the city.

After a few hours, Cal had managed to walk around the city walls without finding an opportunity to get out, until he found a section of the wall with crates stacked to give him the opportunity to climb the wall and jump over.

As Cal was heading for the crates, he heard a voice behind him command, "Hold it right there, turn around and give me your name and purpose for being in the city."

Cal turned around and saw four Crimson soldiers readying their weapons. "The name's Cal, and I am just traveling through."

"You need to be more specific than that."

Cal started to speak, but he saw more Crimson soldiers arrive, and said, "For just visiting, you guys know how to arrange a welcoming party. I'm mighty honored to have such a group come and welcome me."

"If you will not answer, then we will place you under arrest."

"Now, I have already told you why I am here. It's not very kind to arrest a poor old man who has lost his way."

The commanding officer of the bunch looked to the soldier on his right and said, "Bring Major Denthon, tell him we have the agent he is looking for."

The soldier replied with a "Yes Sir," and was off.

Cal looked at the man, his eyes narrowed, and then he smiled brightly, saying, "I guess I had best be off. It sure was mighty fine talkin' with you boys today." Cal started walking off to the left when one of the soldiers came at him to seize him.

Cal spun around and kicked the man hard in his chest. The soldier flew backward, and writhing on the ground clutching his chest. "Get him!" ordered the commanding officer, and all the others charged him. Cal ran, and he was quick.

Through the streets, he outran the soldiers. Other soldiers appeared in front of him. Cal exclaimed, "Where are they coming from!" The chase lasted several minutes until Cal found himself surrounded. The commanding officer came up to Cal, clearly out of breath, grabbed him, and threw him onto the ground. Cal caught himself on his hands and knees, and looked up at the officer and said, "For a trained soldier, your endurance level sure is low. You might want to work on that. I'd hate for the soldiers under you to get a bad opinion of ya."

The officer snarled and kicked Cal as hard as he could in the abdomen. Cal fell over, grimacing in pain. "Keep your mouth shut 'old man.' Take him and lock him up. Make sure he's guarded at all times. General Kein will arrive in three days for interrogation."

11

The Resistance

Two days later Cal was still held in jail when the servant who brought his lunch was not his normal servant. The servant was the merchant who sold him the weapons the day he arrived in town. The merchant unlocked the gate and motioned Cal to come. Cal quietly stepped to the gate and the merchant whispered into his ear, "We have arranged for your escape, but our window of opportunity is only open for a short while, we must hurry."

Cal nodded his understanding and both men crept through the halls quietly. The merchant guided Cal along the halls and through the door in the back. The sun was bright and Cal had to squint his eyes to see clearly. The merchant continued to lead Cal through the alleys and back streets, avoiding the potential Crimson sentries.

"We're almost there. We have received your gear and acquired the horses you were seeking, but we have a mission for you. With the gear you requested and the coin you used, we assume you're headed to Haven." The merchant's face was full of hope and excitement as he stared into Cal's eyes

Cal looked at the man with a discerning look and decided to trust him and said, "Aye, that is my destination, but that's all I can say."

"Good, we hoped as much. I am an officer in the Perri Royal forces. I was sent here to spy out Qunereel's forces. Since Perri has been invaded by the Crimson, I have stayed here and managed to learn of the Resistance.

Not everyone in Qunereel is sympathetic to Shorn Forte and the Crimson Army. The resistance is strong, very organized, and ready to attack. But we cannot do it alone. We desire to let Haven know that if they can organize an open offensive, we are ready to attack from the rear. If you need to locate a local resistance cell, just look for our symbol near a building. The resident will know who to contact." The man then drew a symbol that looked very much like a target, but the center cross had four circles in each corner. Then he continued, "This is our symbol. Remember the resistance is ready, but we can't do it alone. Please pass the word."

Cal looked at the man and said, "If I can do anything, I will. What is your name?"

"My name is Maercen." Maercen looked back in the direction of the jail and saw several soldiers coming out of it. "We must hurry."

The two men ran and remained in the shadows as much as possible. Then Maercen stopped and said, "This is as far I go, but you must keep to the gates, and run to the grove of trees on the north side of the city. There you will find Brennan, the merchant who sold you the cooking supplies. He will have your gear and horses."

Cal looked towards the gates that opened to the grove, "It'll be a tough run, but I should be able to handle it before the Crimsons are aware."

"I don't know about that." Cal turned in horror as he saw Maercen drop to his knees while a Crimson officer withdrew his blade from Maercen's collapsing body. "I plan to kill you here."

Cal kicked dust up into the eyes of the officer. Bent over in agony, the officer ordered the soldiers adjacent to him to capture the prisoner. Cal fought them off with brutal precision and made a run for the gate. An arrow hit the wall just inches in front of him and then using his momentum, he slid to the gate while another arrow struck the wall where he would have been. Cal heard the gallop of several horses in the Crimson cavalry charging. He looked at them with disgust. Quickly climbing to his feet, he sprinted toward the grove, three horses in hot pursuit.

Though he ran swiftly, the leading soldier quickly gained ground on Cal. Cal, expecting a deadly blow of a sword, did a somersault and the blade missed its mark. Cal was quickly back on his feet and continued toward the woods. The three cavalry units turned their mounts around and began a fresh charge. The soldier on the right sheathed his sword and readied his bow. He drew his cord back with a ready arrow and released.

Cal gauged the arrow and realized that the archer's shot was pure and that his momentum didn't allow for a significant course change to avoid the projectile. Hope nearly was exhausted when a white flash rushed by him and the arrow was nowhere to be found. Turning he saw Lady gaining altitude with the arrow clutched in her talons. "It can't be," he whispered. He turned back to the woods and saw Iris charging toward one of the soldiers and a young man firing an arrow. Both found their marks and the three Cavalry quickly turned into one. The one, realizing his party was lost, retreated back to Os.

Cal ran up to Junath, "I told you to give me a week."

Junath's countenance fell at the rebuke, but Cal said, "Come here, boy, well done, well done." Cal embraced him and then said, "Come, we haven't much time before they send reinforcements."

The reunited party of four found Brennen where Maercen said he would be found. Brennen had witnessed the escape and the first thing he asked was the welfare of Maercen.

"He's dead," was Cal's reply.

Brennen clutched his chest in pain of his loss. "He was my best friend," he whispered.

Placing his hand on Brennen's shoulder Cal said, "Come with us, it's not safe here."

"No, there is too much at stake. I must continue our work, but I will certainly be vigilant. Ride hard, my friends, and may we finally see the end of Crimson tyranny."

Cal nodded his head in approval and said, "Farewell, and we will deliver your message to Haven." The two men clasped each other's arms in a salute, and they went their separate ways.

12

Cal's Song

For the next month, Cal led Junath northwest. During that time they continued to train. Junath was very impressed with the increased power of his new bow, and the elegant balance of his new sword. Lady was very loyal to Junath and except to look ahead or hunt, she rarely left his side.

When the party was two days from Anvil Forest, Cal commented, "I am concerned about the forest. I have only ventured near it a handful of times. The locals tell of massive bears that roam the forest; bears that stand twelve feet high when on their hind legs. I just passed it off as a story to scare travelers and little children, but since we cannot go on the east side of the lake, we must go through the forest. Therefore, we need to keep our wits about us. If we don't dawdle, we may only have to spend two nights in the forest and be out the third day. Your training may come in handy. So keep your eyes open."

When they came upon the forest, Junath was awed with its size. It stretched as far as the eye could see. The trees were twice as tall as any tree back in Perri. One peculiar aspect of these trees was their bark or lack thereof. The bases of the trees were shrouded with the natural-looking brown bark, but ten feet up the trunk the bark disappeared and a beautiful ivory white tree grew toward the heavens. Junath let out a soft whistle as he admired the forest of white wooden trees.

"The trees are called Giant Sycamores," Cal informed Junath, seeing the wonder on his face. "But if you really want to see a beautiful forest, this one barely compares to the forest of the North. That forest practically spans the northern stretch of Manähu, stretching from the edge of Davenshire through Tuckshire. However, Forte's war on Tuckshire has left much of the forest on the east barren…"

Cal began to trail off as he began to mention the war on Tuckshire. Junath looked over at Cal and noticed Cal looking off to the north with a cold, bitter, and sad countenance. Junath thought it best to let Cal be alone, but he made a mental note to ask about it later if the time seemed right. Cal barely spoke two words outside of commands to set up camp, and Junath knew something deep was bothering him.

The two sat around the fire in silence and when Junath was about the turn in, he heard Cal begin to hum a melody that was deep, somber, and sounding slightly macabre. When Cal began to sing the words, he realized the depth of Cal's pain.

"There I dwelt long and sweet
with my wife and children three
The children pure, their mother fair
By the fire, I watch all that I care
The morrow I leave to hunt
Known it would be my last, I wouldn't
My children hug my knee
On my lips, did my wife kiss me
When I left, I saw the airships come
So many bombs fell, I lost the sum
I ran home in haste
With fear on my face
Made it home, my horror grew in size
My family dead, by the Crimson Rise."

Cal lowered his head and began to sob, Junath turned from Cal and sat silent. After a couple of minutes, Cal spoke and said, "Shorn killed my family and there was nothing I could have done. How I wish I could have died there with them. I long for the day that Shorn gets what's coming to him. There is no pain greater than seeing your babies lying there lifeless, and you can't do nothing. It is said that Forte was angered by his wife's infidelity with the crown Prince of Tuckshire. He destroyed my family, friends, and neighbors just because he was enraged over his wife! Little is left of Tuckshire. When he attacked, we were blindsided and stood no chance, and his lust for blood hasn't ended."

Cal threw a log into the fire. The wood crackled and orange illuminated ash fluttered into the air. The ash soon lost its fire disappearing into the night sky. He then rose and walked into the woods. Junath realized that he and Cal lost much from Shorn and the Crimson army. Junath thought to himself, "A man can't survive long making enemies like Shorn has. Maybe one day I'll show him." Junath's jaw muscles tensed and his chest burned with pain and anger. Junath turned in and slept, but his dreams only highlighted his hate.

Cal woke Junath up. Cal had his hand over Junath's mouth with a finger over his own mouth to indicate silence. Junath nodded his head in understanding. He noticed that dawn was barely visible. He quietly sat up and Cal pointed his finger down by the water. There was a bear drinking.

The bear was huge. It was nearly twelve feet at the shoulder. He was an odd color with his light brown hair with white and black patches. Junath was familiar with small black and brown bears of Perri. This bear indeed was different and frightening.

At that moment the wind shifted and came from their backs and headed straight toward the bear. Cal grimaced and readied his bow with an arrow knowing what was next. The bear raised his head with alert and sniffed the air. He turned his head toward Junath, Cal, and Iris. The bear bellowed a deep reverberating roar shaking Junath to the core. The horses reared and Cal and Junath quickly dismounted preparing for battle.

Cal leaned down and spoke into Junath's ear saying, "This is not the time to lose your wits boy. Remember your training and ready yourself."

Junath mustered his courage and was able to repress his fear. He knew that he was staring death in its eyes and if he allowed his fear to control him, he would most assuredly see death win. Besides, he had Cal, Iris, and Lady on his side and this was just one bear. A really large bear.

The bear rose to his hind legs and doubled in height. Junath looked around for Lady, but did not see her. He didn't meditate too much on her absence because he knew she was well aware of the situation. An arrow from Cal's bow shot through the air and landed dead center in the bear's chest. The bear roared viciously because of the pain, but he gave no indication that his vitality had even dwindled a fraction. Cal loaded another arrow and shot again, and then again. The bear charged.

Junath managed to load one arrow and fire it before the bear was nearly on them. The bear looked like a pin cushion.

Junath prepared to jump to the left when Iris charged the bear and latched herself onto the bear's throat with her teeth. The bear recoiled and swatted his throat and shook his head violently. Iris was catapulted to the side, but she was quickly back onto her feet. During the delay, Cal repositioned himself to the bear's right flank and ordered Junath to take the left. "Split his attention," Cal yelled.

Junath placed several more arrows into the hide of the bear and Cal twice as many. Junath noticed that Cal was running low on arrows and he knew something must be done quickly if they were to win. Junath pulled his quiver off and yelled at the bear. When the bear's attention was on Junath, he threw the quiver of arrows toward Cal and drew his sword. By the look on Cal's face, Junath knew he was not happy. The bear was full of rage and ready to kill, and Cal continued to load arrows into its hide. The ravenous bear kept its sight on Junath.

Junath made a jab at the bear, but the bear lunged for Junath and knocked him to the ground. Junath kept stabbing at the bear until its paw swatted Junath's hand with horrendous strength. The sword dislodged and flew to Junath's right, sticking into the ground ten feet away. Cal began to yell to distract the bear, but the bear's focus was on his prey. He roared violently in Junath's face and saliva dripped onto Junath. Just as the bear was about to chomp down on his dinner, Lady flew in and attacked the bear. Realizing Lady arrived for the rescue, he scrambled toward his sword hoping to reposition himself to engage the bear again.

Cal was already attacking the bear with his sword and Lady was again in the trees. Iris, by Cal's side, was ready to attack at the opportune time. Junath's courage was as strong as ever, though he was near death, his adrenaline was pulsating through his body. His reaction was to fight.

Junath circled around until he was behind the bear. He rushed up and sliced deeply through the bear's left hamstring. The result was instant, the bear stumbled backward and his leg went out from under him. Cal pressed his attack noticing the bear's weakened state and Iris latched again onto the bear's throat. Junath climbed on top of the wounded bear and reached his neck. Junath shoved his sword into the base of the bear's head. The bear's violent temper was immediately tamed.

Junath could hear the vibration of a growl deep inside the bear, but all that the bear did was stumble to the right and collapse with a large thud. Junath rolled into the fall and sprang onto his feet. The bear was dead.

When Junath realized it was over, his legs gave way and he fell to the ground exhausted. Cal rushed over to Junath to make sure he was all right.

"Junath, can you hear me? Junath!" Fear was written all over his face.

Junath slowly opened his eyes and saw Cal looking worriedly over him and Junath began to smile. Looking at Cal he said, "I thought you said they were only twelve feet when standing?"

Cal didn't hesitate but said, "I reckon they told me about the females."

Junath slowly got to his feet and asked, "So how'd I do?"

Cal looked at him hard and stern for what seemed minutes, but then a smile was broad on his face and he said, “Looks like you will do.” Both began to laugh

Cal continuing said, “Come. We have a long road ahead of us, and I don’t want to find out if this guy has any brothers.”

13

An Unlikely Visitor

Over the three weeks, Junath and Cal traveled northwest along the Anvil River. They continued on the west side of the Dark Wadi. Cal contemplated whether or not to stop and resupply in Phip before they crossed the mountains and entered Haven, but decided to trudge through and end the exodus before someone or something got them.

Cal continued to train and study with Junath, teaching him the art of tracking, archery, and swordsmanship. Since the bear attack, Cal pressed on Junath to anticipate the next step. "Staying two or three steps ahead of your enemy will be the difference between life or death," Cal said. Junath put it into practice as much as possible. As he sparred with Cal on their downtime to allow the horses to rest, he tried to anticipate Cal's next two or three moves. After several days he found that he was beginning to match Cal more efficiently.

Cal noticed too and said, "Junath, you shall soon surpass me in swordsmanship. You have true natural talent. Keep honing your skill and you could be the best."

When they were a day from Phip, Junath could hear Cal humming the melody to the song he sang the night before the bear attacked. Junath closed his eyes and remembered Cal telling him briefly about the death of his family, which reminded Junath of his own father's sacrifice.

"Cal?"

"Hmm?"

"Can you tell me about your family?"

Cal was quieted by the inquiry, but after a few minutes, he decided to speak.

"We lived about ten miles outside of Sarena. My wife's name was Liza, and she had hair red as fire. If she wanted, her attitude could match. Both of us were quite stubborn, but she was indeed a good wife. My home was always a more desirable place than anywhere else. Most men I talk to would rather hang out at the tavern or the hunter's lodge than stay at home with their women. But me and my Liza truly loved one another.

"We had two children. My boy was nine and my girl was six. They both had their mother's red hair. Though Alana's was more on the auburn side than the fire. Felinix couldn't wait until he went hunting with me. I was waiting until he was twelve.

"A little over a year ago, I took leave of my home. Iris and I were heading out for our hunt. I looked at my family and all were in tears. They hated it when I left. My children would hug me and I would have to pry them off. Oh, how I loved them. I pretended not to be, but I wanted to cry like them. Once I was a good hour away from home is when I would allow myself the tears. Two hours in, there was a ridge from where I could see Sarena and my home. That day, though, would be different.

"All went like clock-work and we did our normal rituals. However, when I left and made it to the ridge, I turned to see a nightmare. In the distance, I saw hundreds of dark clouds. I took a double-take and wondered what it could mean. Iris and I waited to see. The clouds came closer to Sarena. It was a fleet of those airships created by Shorn Forte. As they approached, they dropped a strange weapon that exploded. My gut became an instant knot. I sprinted home.

"When I arrived, it was too late. Sarena was devastated. I ran home and my house was cinders. I found…found them huddled together. Liza holding my babies."

"What a sad story, 'bout near made me cry." Cal and Junath spun around at the sound of the voice. They turned and to their horror, it was a squad of Crimson soldiers.

Cal whispered to Junath, "Get ready to run. I will distract them and when I raise my hand you bolt to the woods." To the soldiers, he said with a smile, "Greetings, didn't know we had an audience. You didn't let me get to the best part."

"And what would that be Tucksan?" The soldier who spoke was dressed like the commanding officer that ordered Junath's father to be killed, but by his voice, he obviously was not the same man.

Still, with the same smile, Cal replied, "The fact that I die fighting those who killed my family." Cal's countenance changed to hardened steel and he raised his hand to draw his sword and Junath bolted into the woods. Then from a heavy blow to the head he fell to the ground and everything went black.

Junath woke beside a fire, bound to a wooden pole. Beside him, Cal was alive, alert and watching Junath. He too was bound to a pole beside the fire.

"It's about time. You've been out for hours. I didn't think he hit you that hard."

"I feel like I've been run over by an ox."

"I told you to wait for my signal, I was going to distract them, but no, mister-jumpy-pants has to run the moment I begin my plan."

"Really? You told me to run when you raised your hand. I ran when you raised your hand."

"I said I was going to distract them. I wasn't ready for you to run."

"Well, you should have made that a little clearer."

Cal and Junath continued to bicker back and forth until a Crimson soldier yelled for them to be quiet.

In a whisper, Junath asked, "What about Lady and Iris?"

"They escaped."

"Well, that's good news. Why didn't they warn us?"

"That's a good question. She's usually more on top of things, but so am I, and yet here we are."

"How do you propose we get out of here?" Junath said.

With a scowl, Cal said, "I don't have high hopes, but this unit seems to be on the more undisciplined side of the spectrum. I think we wait until we are removed from the poles and plan to fight our way out. That's the best I got."

"Sounds like a good plan to get ourselves killed."

"Well you asked, and that's what I am thinking. Don't worry, either we'll be killed, delivered to Crimson high command, or a path of escape will present itself. I've been watching this unit and I think something will present itself. Plus we have Iris and Lady working something out." And under his breath, he added, "I hope."

"I said keep it quiet!" The soldier walked over and kicked Cal in the side.

Cal winced and looked up at the soldier and said with a forced smile, "Thank you kindly, I was beginning to think you forgot about us. It's been a while since someone shoved a good boot into my ribs. My daddy always said a man will always need a good pair of boots." The soldier kicked him again and commanded him to close his mouth.

When the soldier had walked away, Junath whispered to Cal, "I don't think that is what your father had in mind."

"You think?"

Both Cal and Junath rested in silence and were wondering what the morrow would bring when they heard Iris howl. Cal and Junath became instantly alert. Seconds later, they heard Lady vocalize her presence as well in the sky above. They looked at each other wondering what this meant when suddenly a unit of cavalry stormed the camp. Their armor was polished steel, accessed with a rich blue and green. The uniform was completely foreign to Junath. He heard the Crimson commander crying for the soldiers to take arms and fight. It was chaos and Junath and Cal just had to wait it out. Junath could see both Iris and Lady fighting. The Crimsons continued to resist, but it was futile. Within five minutes, the Crimsons were vanquished and this new army commanded the camp.

Iris came and nuzzled Cal inspecting him for wounds. Lady landed in front of Junath. She turned her head and looked at the new soldier dismount his horse and head over to Junath and Cal. He obviously was of high rank and most likely the commander of the unit that attacked. His armor was very similar to the others, but his helm was highly decorated with blue plumes where the others were just plain. On his helmet was etched an elaborate design of flowers and vines, but the image that stood out was a tree centered on both sides of the helm displaying thick deep roots. His shield was likewise decorated, but on the tree was an opened book. Girded round his waist was an intricately woven belt that held an ornate sheath containing his sword. His horse too was decorated elegantly in a blue and green blanket. The horse's armor was etched with similar patterns as her master's.

The officer approached Junath and inspected him with a very meticulous and curious eye. He stroked his thick brown beard and kneeling to the ground sliced the ropes binding Junath's hands. The man stood and reached his hand out to Junath and said, "I'd wager you have quite a story for me since you seem to have earned the trust of my father's owl."

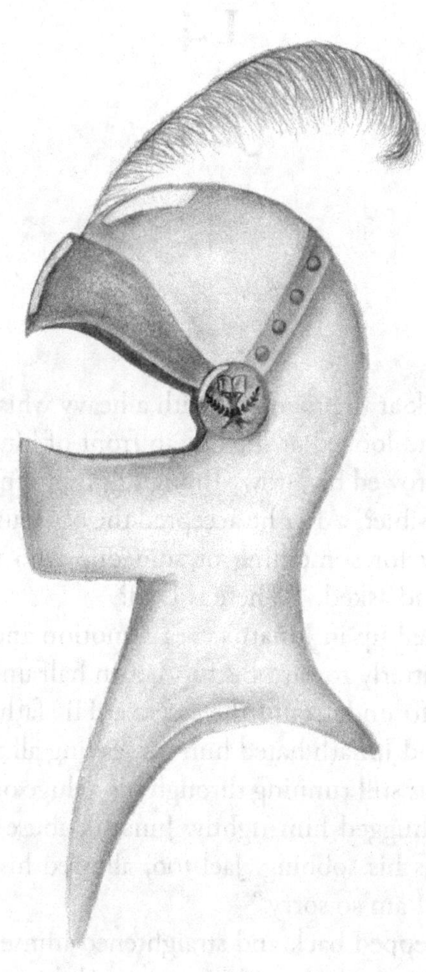

14

Jael

Junath stared back at the man and with a heavy whisper said, "Jael?"

Jael paused and looked at the boy in front of him with wonder. His lips pursed and furrowed his brow. Though dumbfounded he managed to say, "Is it really possible?" After he accepted the obvious, he looked around searching intensely for something or someone who was not there. Jael looked at Junath and asked, "Where is Dad?"

Angry tears welled up in Junath's eyes. Emotion and anger spewed out and Junath fired bitterly toward his brother in half unintelligible phrases, but Jael managed to understand the essence. His father was dead by the Crimson's hand, and Junath hated him for leaving all those years ago.

While Junath was still running through his deluge of verbal attacks, Jael grabbed him and hugged him tightly. Junath's abuse ended and all that could be heard was his sobbing. Jael too, allowed his tears to fall freely, saying, "I'm sorry, I am so sorry."

Junath finally stepped back and straightened himself, allowing himself to look at his brother perhaps with not so much bitterness. Jael looked at his brother and a series of questions began to form in his mind but he only asked, "Why are you here?"

Junath began to tell him all that had happened. How Seren came home from the town meeting, demanding that he get ready to go, the armor Seren put on, the wanted poster, the parchment, and the flight into the delta. He mentioned Lady's attack on Finister Kein, at which Jael, with a harsh bite in his words, said under his breath, "Serves him right. Always getting into something too big for his britches." Junath told him how he met Cal and Iris and about their training and the travels up to when they were finally caught by the Crimson's army.

"What a story indeed," Jael said after Junath was finished. "I suppose you are interested in hearing my story. Hopefully, it will explain a few things. Come and let's sit and enjoy a meal together. I find a meal warms the soul and opens the hearts of both parties toward one another."

After they settled down, Jael began his tale. "After Mom died, it was very tough on the farm. We were barely making it. One day some travelers came down from Qunereel, this is before Shorn's coup against the king, and they were talking about the money that can be made in the mines. I felt that I could leave and earn some money to send back to the farm to help out, which I did. Without me, Dad would not have to support me, just you, and with the extra income out of the mines, he could have better peace of mind. I thought it best, but perhaps it was not the best choice.

"However, had I not gone there, then I would not be who I am today. Much happened to me in Qunereel. I proved to be a very resourceful and innovative worker. I designed many machines that enhanced and simplified the work in the mines. Some in the ranks of the king thought that my mind could be put to better use than slaving away. They offered me a position in the Ministry of Science. While in the Ministry of Science, I was also offered a scholarship to attend their university. And that is where I met Isabella."

Upon hearing her name, Junath said, "Dad said something the night he died about having nothing to with Isabella. What was he talking about?"

Jael gave a sigh and said, "This is where the story gets interesting. Isabella and I fell in love. Now, this was welcomed and everyone was happy. But it was at this time the monarchy of Qunereel was about to be uprooted. Shorn Forte was a high general in the Qunereelian army, but after his wife left him, he became a violent usurper. In one week of bloody revolts, he was the supreme dictator. Unfortunately, Isabella is Shorn's youngest daughter.

"Of course I was able to keep my post in the Ministry of Science, and I tried to leave the politics alone. However, I discovered this gas in the western portions of Qunereel. I knew it was useful and found a way to harness it in pouches. This gave birth to the development of the airships. Shorn used my technology to create warships that could drop explosives. And when he used this weapon on Tuckshire and decimated that nation, I had to finally speak up."

Junath shot a look over to Cal, and he remembered the song Cal sang just before the ambush. Now, apparently, Jael had a hand in that attack.

Jael continued, "I couldn't bear the thought that my work was being used to kill, without mercy, innocent people. I became very vocal in my opposition to Shorn's lust. He threw me into prison and ordered my execution at the next sunrise. However, that night Isabella came to my rescue, broke me out, and we escaped together to Haven. It was a difficult escape and journey, but we made it. When we arrived we were married and we have a daughter, Tirzah. Oh, you'll love her Junny.

"While in Haven, with my knowledge of the Crimson army and government, the Chancellor appointed me an advisor. After proving my worth, he commissioned me as a commander in the army. We were out doing reconnaissance when Lady found me and led us here."

At that moment, one of Jael's officers approached with the sealed parchment in his hand. He handed it to Jael and he inspected the two royal seals from Thea and Perri. A whisper escaped his lips as he said, "Finally." Then he said out loud, "I'm so glad these Crimson dogs didn't have the sense to open this before now."

He slowly broke the seals and unfurled the parchment, closing his eyes as if afraid of what he might find written in the document before him. He opened his eyes and spent several minutes studying the text. Relief seemed to wash over him.

Jael looked at his officer and said, "Perri and Thea have amassed their troops in the Great Pine Forest. They also have a large number of refugees from Tuckshire who have joined their ranks. Altogether, they have mustered 75,000 men of war. They agree to an alliance. You take the rest of the men and make haste to join the army and prepare the men to attack the Crimson rear."

"Jael," Junath said, "Cal and I have met with others between here and Perri who call themselves the Resistance." Junath then described the symbol to look for and mentioned Brennen by name.

Jael relayed the information to his officer and ordered him to find as many Resistance fighters on their way.

"It shall be done, Sir," was his reply. The officer then commanded the soldiers to rest that night and to be prepared to break camp two hours before dawn. Jael took the parchment and burned it in the fire. Junath and Jael spent time becoming more acquainted. Junath told his story from home up to the camp. Jael did the same.

That night at dinner, Jael informed Junath and Cal on the current movements of the Crimson army and the strategies Haven was utilizing to mount a defense. The strongest weapon the Crimsons had were the airships, so Jael designed a projectile weapon that could be fired and explode on a timer. The blast would send thousands of shredded metal flakes into the air with the hopes that the weapon would puncture the airship's balloons and cause them to fall from the sky. Unfortunately, Haven did not have the resources as Qunereel, but they did manage to harvest a gas similar from the Sanctuary Mountains that could be used like the gas in the Crimson airships. However, Qunereel would certainly have the advantage.

The next morning when Junath awoke, most of Jael's men had already departed. Jael, Cal, Junath, and three other soldiers left camp and made it to Phip in less than a day's ride.

Phip was a comfortable small city. It rested on a plateau near a river and if you looked East you could see the beautiful Geor Desert. To enter the city, there were four gates. Each gate had a guard shack and was manned constantly by two guards both day and night. Though they were not enemies, Geor and Sprinx were not exactly on the best of terms with each other. Therefore Geor fortified Phip and had a small regiment of soldiers. As they approached the guards, Iris stopped and whimpered. Cal looked at her and said, "What is it, girl?"

Something made Iris completely uncomfortable and Cal looked to Jael and said, "I trust this wolf with my life. She's knows something is wrong here."

Jael replied, "I was just here the other day. Everything was normal."

"Well if Iris isn't going in, then I'm not either. We'll wait for ya'll to come out and then regroup."

Jael, slightly aggravated, agreed and proceeded to enter. Junath stayed with his brother, but Lady wasn't too keen on entering either.

Since Geor was an ally with Haven, the guards allowed Jael and his party to enter unhindered. As they crossed the threshold, Junath saw concern wash over Jael's face as he looked back at the guard. Jael did not offer any commentary.

Inside the city, Jael huddled with his men and said, “We’ve got three days before we reach the southern pass. I’m going to meet with the city administrator, but I need you to replenish our supplies.” He handed them a sack of coin. Then he added, “Keep your eyes open, something’s not quite right. Perhaps Cal and his wolf were right.”

The officer on Jael’s right who had dark hair, a thin black mustache that curled on the ends, and a small patch of black hair on his chin replied, “Yes sir, I agree. The air has indeed soured.”

“Good, we will meet here in one hour, if we’re not back in two, then you better come and find us, maybe check the prison first.” Jael gave a half chuckle, but Junath could tell it was a vain attempt at a joke to conceal the seriousness of his command. With the confirmation of the orders, the three soldiers left Jael and Junath to gather the supplies.

Jael turned to Junath and said, “Come, let’s see what’s going on here.”

The Governor’s Hall was a modest building. It wasn’t too extravagant but decorated enough to reveal it wasn’t just an ordinary office. Before they walked up the steps to the door, Junath whispered to Lady, “Hang out here until we get back.”

Lady flew off his arm and perched herself atop the pinnacle of the Hall building. As they entered the Governor’s Hall, a butler approached them and asked, “Good afternoon, Commander Symp, how can I be of assistance?”

Jael said, “I have come to seek an audience with Governor Tion”

“Yes sir. I will let Lord Tion know you are present.”

Jael bowed his head and the butler headed down the hall towards the reception room. After he was out of earshot, Jael leaned toward Junath and said, “Something’s definitely not right, this butler, who I know has been in service to this house for the better part of a decade, just called Governor Tion ‘Lord.’”

Junath confused, asked the question, “What does that mean? How can it prove something isn’t right? In Perri, all city officials can be called ‘Lord.”

Jael leaned in and said, “Yeah, but in Geor, ‘Lord’ is a term strictly reserved for the king. Tion isn’t the king by any definition.”

Junath simply replied, “Oh. Let me send a word to Cal. We may need his help.”

“I think you’re right. Make it quick.”

Junath quickly turned and took a piece of paper and scribbled, "Keep your eyes open, we don't like it here. Looks like trouble." When he stepped outside he called Lady and she lighted on his arm. "Lady, take this note and find Cal. Now fly!" She took off and headed out of town. When Junath walked back in, Jael was still standing, waiting on the butler.

After a few minutes, the butler came back and said, "Lord Tion will now see you."

As they entered the reception hall, the room was not what Junath was expecting. The walls were simple gray wood and the official table was a modestly formed desk. But the most eye-catching were the six Crimson soldiers in the room with Governor Tion. "High Commander Symp, what a joyous surprise. Though I suspect you won't find much joy in this unfortunate situation. But as for me, when Forte learns of your capture, I will be made Ruler of Geor and Haven both."

15

The Way of Escape

"You're a traitor, Governor Tion. And Shorn Forte is not the man you should ally yourself with. He's vindictive and violent. He'll have your head on a platter if you just sneeze incorrectly." Jael's face hardened and his eyes pierced through Tion's confident manner.

Tion squirmed in his chair, and clearing his throat he tried to regain his confidence and said, "Jael, you are the one mistaken. A new era is dawning in our world. Times are changing and we must change with it. You hold on to your ideals of Haven which have always made me sick. When a man rules, why give it up? Your elections are pathetic and will be the ruin of your beloved country. Forte exemplifies the power that all men desire. It burns in me too, and I would be the foolish one if I stayed locked in arms with a failing Geor monarchy and an idealistic Haven democracy. This is the Crimson Rise!"

"Perhaps you are right Tion, but Forte is not ushering in an era of peace and prosperity, but one of death and decay. The Crimson Rise is built on the blood of innocents. It's cruel and heartless."

"Oh Jael, you're so short-sighted. But you will see, you will see." Tion spread his hands, pointing to the two Crimson soldiers and said, "Allow my friends to show you two to your 'room.'" Tion chuckled at the jest.

The soldiers, dressed in their black uniforms, stood and began walking toward Junath and Jael. Junath and Jael readied themselves and the fight began quickly. Though outnumbered, both Junath and Jael held their own and made their way down the corridor. The door was near, but another band of soldiers had gathered. There was no way to escape. Jael said, "Lower your weapon, we're outmatched." Conceding to his brother's command, Junath lowered his sword. The soldiers knocked both of them unconscious.

Junath woke shackled to a prison wall and whispered, "Man, I need to stop waking up like this." Jael was next to him. Above them was a small barred window, which seemed to be facing West. Groaning, he asked, "How long were we out?"

"I'm guessing a couple of hours," was Jael's whispered reply.

They heard the lock on the door become free with the rattling of keys. They heard the rhythmic cadence of boots against the stone. A man's dark form then walked into the cell. As the little light from the window revealed more of the soldier, Junath deepened further into despair as he saw the scarred face of Finister Kein step into the light.

"Well, well, well…Brothers together again. I'm surprised the runt was able to survive up to this point. And you Jael, you look like you've made a name for yourself in that poor excuse of a nation. Too bad we're about to wipe it out. The Crimson Army is encamped as we speak just on the east side of the Geor Canyon ready to invade."

Looking squarely into Kein's eyes, Jael said, "A free people will fight with a lion's heart. Coercion may make people follow in fear, but their hearts aren't in it. One man in Haven is equal to twenty of yours."

"Haven will have their chance to prove their mettle soon enough." Finister moved toward Junath and walked up to him. He leaned into the boy's face. His breath was revolting. It was somewhere between a dead animal and onions, but Junath did not flinch nor act repulsed. "Take a long look at my scars. I salivate at the thought of you paying your debt to me." Finister took out a long knife and held the blade against Junath's face. Junath just stared into his eyes.

"Stop it, Kein, your fight is with me," Jael said concerned for Junath.

"What, Jael, you afraid I will do this?" Finister drew the knife across Junath's left cheek, drawing a steady flow of blood. Junath clinched his eyes and teeth, but then with that steady gaze, looked Finister in the eyes once more.

Jael began thrashing against his chains and managed to lift his legs far enough to kick Finister and made him lose his balance. Finister stumbled but did not fall. He sternly walked over to Jael and kicked him hard and square in the gut. Jael let out a harsh groan.

Finister leaned over to Jael and said, "At sunrise, you both will hang, but first you will have to watch your brother writhe in the noose. Oh, how I will then revel in your death." He leaned in closer and whispered into Jael's ear, "Then Isabella will be mine."

Jael began to thrash again, but Finister backed away quickly, turned, and marched out the door. A guard locked the door behind him. Jael and Junath again were alone.

Jael looked over at Junath and saw the blood still flowing down his cheek. He said, "I'm sorry, Junny, I really am."

"I hate that man... I want to kill him. I will kill him."

Jael was taken aback by Junath's darkness, but he allowed Junath's words to float on the air without a reply. He too had no love for Finister Kein.

After a couple of hours had passed both Jael and Junath became alert at the sound of a loud thud at the door of their cell. Then they heard the keys rattling again with another thud accompanied by a frustrated but familiar grumbling, "How in the world are these keys attached?" Junath smiled to hear Cal's voice, though the smile quickly vanished when it caused the cut on his face to scream in pain. When the door opened, Iris rushed in checking on Junath. She whined when she noticed his wound. Cal came in right behind her.

"Time is of the essence...whoa, Junath, that'll be a nice looking scar one day. You'll have to tell me how you got it when we all get out of here alive." Cal took the keys and released Junath and Jael from their shackles.

Jael asked Cal, "Do you know where the others are?"

"Aye, I found them first and they're helping keep an eye out for other guards."

"Where are our horses?"

"Hmm, probably at the stables, but that place is guarded as tough as a mama bear with her cubs."

Jael sighed but then said, "Well, let's head that way and see how to cross

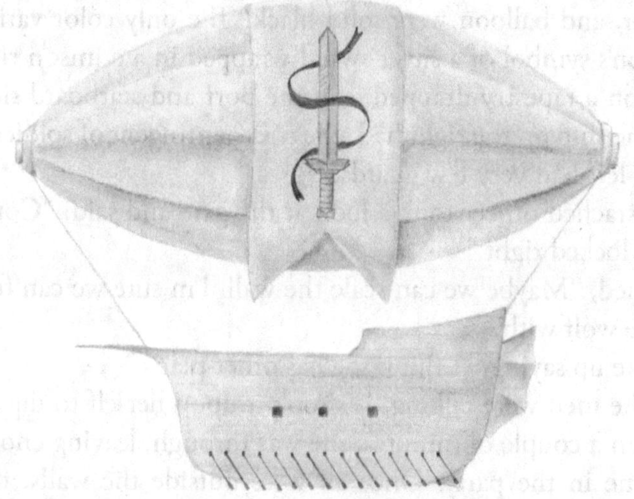

that bridge when we get there."

The three of them rendezvoused with the other soldiers. They escaped the prison, and Junath was comforted to see Lady perched on the pinnacle of a nearby public building. Now their new quest was to escape Phip. Hiding in the shadows, they all scurried to the stables. Sure enough, a heavily armed squadron of men was on patrol watching over the horses.

Cal, seeing the difficult path ahead, leaned over to Jael and whispered, "There may be another option, let me see what you think."

Following Cal's lead, they all navigated the alleys and crates and arrived at the East Gate. Sneaking up on the sentries and knocking them out, they looked through the gate. Cal pointed and said, "Any ideas how it works, master builder?"

Jael confidently said, "Hmm, yes, yes I do."

Junath, looking out in the moonlight, saw two airships about 50 yards apart. The ships' hulls were like a standard wooden ship bound to the water. But out of the hull of the vessels were forty large leather-finned paddles shaped much like the fins on a fish. On the rear of both ships were sizeable leather-finned rudders to steer the boats through the air. Ballast was used to help raise and lower the crafts. Above the ships were an elongated balloon filled with a gas that allowed the boats to float in the air. The material was a patchwork of fabric that was completely sealed, preventing the gas from escaping. The balloons were attached to the ships by a series of nets fastened to the hull of the ships. Each craft, including the hull, fins, rudder, and balloon were solid black. The only color variation was the Crimson's symbol of a silver sword wrapped in a crimson ribbon embroidered on a tapestry drapped over the port and starboard sides of the balloon. The ship on the right had a heavier contingent of soldiers, but the one on the left had very few guards.

The mustached officer took a look at the gate and said, "Commander, this gate is locked tight."

Jael replied, "Maybe we can scale the wall. I'm sure we can find a rope to hoist the wolf with."

Cal spoke up saying, "I think she has other plans."

While the men were talking, Iris took it upon herself to dig under the gate. Within a couple of minutes, she was through, leaving enough room for each one in the party. Once all were outside the walls, they made their way to the dirigible on the left. Jael and the three soldiers, staying concealed, rushed ahead to incapacitate the guards on patrol. Afterward, Cal, Junath, Iris, and Lady made their way to the ramp leading into the fuselage.

Moving quickly behind them, Jael said, "We'll make our way to the helm, but we must be careful to clear the storage rooms of any men." But as they moved through the ship, they found no one until they came to the helm. There they saw two more guards.

Cal drew his bow and shot one while Iris viciously attacked the second. Jael jumped to the large wooden wheel and called for the soldiers to cut the ballast. The ship began to rise and the sensation was immediate. Junath's legs felt like putty. It wasn't long until his stomach churned. Jael saw his brother's discomfort and said, "Here try this, it helps settle my stomach when I'm on one of these things." He handed him some dried tangy root that had been cured with sugar. Once Junath's stomach settled, it dawned on him that he was flying. The excitement was nearly overwhelming and in short order, he found his legs.

"Captain, I'm going to use the mountains to guide me, but if you can check the navigator's charts and find me a heading it will make our quest that much quicker."

"Aye, sir," said the man with the mustache and goatee.

Within a couple of minutes, the captain called out a heading of 300 degrees and Jael turned accordingly to align the compass next to the helm. Junath was amazed at how natural Jael was at flying the ship.

"Cal and Junath, keep an eye on that other airship, let me know if it makes any movements," Jael commanded as he guided the airship on its course. Junath and Cal rushed to the rear deck to see what was going on. Being night it was difficult for Junath to see, but the moon did allow them enough exposure to tell general movements. Junath saw in an instant that the airship had taken off and was heading right for them.

Yelling over his shoulder, Junath called back to Jael saying, "It's on its way and it is gaining on us."

Junath heard Jael offer an aggravated complaint and then said, "We need every available man on the oars now! We're severely underhanded and Kein will have a full crew on that ship. Let's get as much altitude as possible. By the looks of the clouds, we may just hit favorable winds higher up."

Within half an hour, Junath heard a large whistling sound that ended in a cracking thud. The airship rocked to the port side causing a sudden loss of balance for the men. When Junath regained his legs, he rushed over to the starboard side and saw a large iron rod sticking out of the hull of the ship.

Jael said, "Those are ballista, large powerful arrows, and he has more where that came from. If he hits our gas cells with a few good hits, we're done! You need to row now."

At that moment Junath heard the whistling again, but this time it didn't hit the hull but slammed into the soldier next to the captain. Junath heard his scream as he went flying across the deck and over the port side, disappearing into the darkness.

"Everyone to the stern ballista, Captian Regi, give Cal and Junath a crash course in ballista mechanics, I'll keep us a moving target."

"Understood, Commander."

Captain Regi coached Junath and Cal on how to load, crank, and fire the massive bow. "This will be all you need to know to keep us flying tonight. I make sure our ballista arrows hit their mark as long as you keep them loaded."

Junath and Cal were a little clumsy at first but after their third arrow, they were getting their system down. Junath could hear the whistle of the arrows as they left, but the tone was deeper and richer than the sound from the arrows from Kein's ship.

"Are any of our shots hitting their ship?" Junath asked.

"We certainly have the advantage of being higher, but I can only confirm that I've hit their hull once, and he's still coming hard. Keep 'em coming, young master."

It didn't take long lifting and carrying those large iron arrows before Junath was feeling exhausted. His arms were begging to rest, but he kept pressing forward. He laid the ninth arrow onto the large wooden crossbow and just before he called, "Ready," he felt a strong tailwind burst from behind the ship and the airship lurched forward, causing the three to stumble. Captain Regi fell on the lever to release the arrow, but at the same time jolted the device. All three looked over the rail to watch the arrow fly. To Junath it seemed as if it were slow motion, but the arrow flew as perfectly as ever and entered two of the three gas cells of Kein's ship. Its forward motion was immediately stopped and Junath watched as the ship sank backward and then begin to spiral down into the darkness.

"We got 'em!" Junath's excitement was uncontainable.

"Aye, sir, the boy is right, the last arrow crippled their ship and we are in the clear." Captain Regi replied.

Jael looked at the men and a grin grew on his face while he said, "Well done, well done."

Cal collapsed, worn out. Junath took a seat next to him against the rail.

Jael called out, "Captain Regi, you, Cal, and Junath go find some bunks. Sergeant Byers and I will continue maintaining our heading. You can relieve us at sun up."

Two decks below, they found their bunks. Junath chose a hammock and was off to sleep before he had time to reminisce about the day.

16

The Southern Pass

The sun rose brightly the next morning, the sky was clear, and the air was cool. Junath's eyes sprang open, and then he rolled out of the hammock, stood, and took in a deep breath. He walked out to the deck and approached the rail. Looking out across the horizon he saw everything and it was beautiful. Lady flew and landed next to him, and he said to her, "What a view you have. I never thought I would get to see it too."

"Junny, if you think the desert is a sight to behold, check out the other side and see the mountains," Jael said as he walked up behind Junath, placing his hands on his shoulders. Junath did as he said and looked out west and saw the mountains reach into the skies with majestic pride. They were grey and green and massive. All the mountains grouped together, creating a granite family. Large ones and small ones with valleys and peaks stretching for miles.

With a humbled sigh, Junath said, "They are so big."

"And these are the small ones. Once we reach the Southern Pass, you will begin to see the glory of the mountains and still farther north, they get even more majestic."

Junath thought to himself, "Majestic, that's the word for these, majestic."

"Who wants breakfast?" Cal came up from the decks below carrying biscuits and cured ham. "Iris and I found the cook's kitchen. With a nose like hers and a stomach like mine, we were destined to find it."

"Yeah, I'm starved," Junath replied

Reaching for a sandwich Jael said, "I do believe I can eat too."

After breakfast, Captain Regi took the helm, and Junath and Cal sat down to the oars. It was a long day of laborious work, but they made good time with the tailwinds pushing them forward. At midday, Cal and Junath took a rest.

Captain Regi walked up to Junath and laid a map down with a round compass. "Thought you might like a lesson on navigation. It's always been my favorite lesson."

"Absolutely!" Cal went to find more biscuits and ham.

"So here's your map. North, east, south, and west are here, here, here, and here. So line up your map with the terrain relative to you. See the rivers here on the map? If you look over the rail, you will see those very rivers.

"Then lay your compass down, it will point north. Measure the angle of the needle pointing north with the point on the map you want to go. Once you have that measurement, you've got your heading. Then, over here by the helm is another compass. Using the compass and the prow of the ship to make the angle you discovered, you will head in the direction you want, barring wind correction of course."

Junath studied the map and the compass for a moment and then said, "Thank you, Captain. I know you oversimplified it for me, but thank you. Getting to ride on this ship is getting more fascinating all the time."

After about an hour, Cal and Iris finally made it back up, but they weren't carrying biscuits and ham, but boiled potatoes, oranges, a slab of beef jerky.

"The ranger brings us a feast!" Captain Regi said.

"Well, I figured 'why not?'"

The day and the night went smoothly, but about three in the morning, the winds changed and started to come from the north. All hands were requested to row. Before Junath sat down to row, his brother took a moment to teach him about winds saying, "Junny, it may be a clear day, but there are a few clouds. What do you notice about them?"

Junath studied them for a moment and then answered, "They're not all moving the same direction or speed."

"That's correct. See, winds won't blow in the same direction or speed, but there are layers. The trick to flying these ships is to keep an eye on which layer is most favorable to you."

Jael descended to a lower altitude where the winds were not as strong. By lunchtime, the Southern Pass was in view.

Taking a break, Junath leaned out over the bow and saw amongst the mountains a large gap. The mountains made an abrupt end. Some were sheared through their center and after about a mile of nothing, the mountains started again as abruptly as they ended.

In awe, Junath asked, "How can that be?"

"We're not sure. No one knows. The history annals only mention their existence, but not how the passes got there."

"Passes? You mean there are others?"

"Yeah, to enter Haven is a very difficult quest. If you are coming by land, only three passes exist, the Northern Pass, the Central Pass, and the Southern Pass. The Sanctuary Mountains are high and extremely dangerous to trek across except through the passes. Haven keeps the three passes heavily guarded."

As they approached the Southern Pass, Junath continued to be in wonder about the lack of mountains through the leveled gap. When he first

heard of the Southern Pass he expected maybe a trail through the mountains, but the mountains were simply just missing. They slowly sailed into the chiseled valley. After a few hours, they saw a large stone wall that spanned the entire width of the path and scaled up the sides of the mountains hundreds of feet. In the center of the stone wall was a large ornate oak gate supported by polished steel. Jael landed and all vacated the airship. As they approached the gate, Jael called out the customary greeting, "Ahoy, may your strength prove steadfast knowing your labor is not in vain."

A reply came from the other side, "May your strength prove as equally steadfast. You may approach the gate."

They all walked up to the wooden door and a sliding window opened. A man peered through it. "Ahh, Commander Symp, welcome back. And with new faces, it would seem." He turned around and yelled, "Release the locks!"

Junath heard the large clanking sound of internal locks dislodging and then the oak door swung slowly open, pushed by five men.

Jael looked to his two soldiers and said, "Bring the airship over the wall. Meet us on the other side. We'll rest tonight in safety."

As Captain Regi and Sergeant Byers turned to go back to the airship, Jael, Junath, Cal, Iris, and Lady all entered the gate.

Expecting to exit on the other side of the wall, Junath found himself in the heart of the wall. Inside, he saw an elaborate system of chains and gears that controlled the locking mechanism for the large oak door. As they walked through the edifice, Jael explained that the walls were 50 feet thick. Small garrisons could be housed inside the walls, and strategically spaced out on the surface of the wall were eyelets to shoot arrows through. Again, Jael had to admit they were clueless about how these walls came to be. Except for a few maintenance instructions, these walls were a mystery.

When they made it out of the wall, Junath walked into a village built between the mountainsides with an active market through the center. Looking down the path, Junath saw that the mountains tapered off. The smells engulfed Junath and he was reminded of the market in Eisen. He continued to walk through the market seeing many trinkets, fruits, vegetables, and meat vendors.

"This way, Junny," said Jael as he veered off to the right.

Jael led the group to the commander's quarters. "We'll rest here." Jael pulled out a couple of cots, pillows, and a few blankets.

Jael continued, "It's imperative that we make an early start. Tomorrow we will need to ride to Palace Home to let the Chancellor know that war is knocking on the door.

17

The Western Gale

"Junny, it's rise and shine." Junath groaned briefly at his brother's command. He could not remember when he had slept in such peace, and he was a little unwilling to let it pass. He finally roused from his slumber.

With a large yawn, Junath said, "I'm coming, give me a minute." Junath scratched his belly and then he perked right up at the smell of breakfast.

Cal was already by the fire and helping prepare the meal. Eggs, bacon, sliced bread with butter, and an interesting fruit that Junath was not familiar with. The fruit was a pasty orange color with a strange rib pattern on the surface. He took one and looked inquisitively at it.

"It's called a cornamen. It grows on the coast of Haven, and it is rather tasty." Jael could tell Junath was clueless about the fruit before him.

Junath peeled off the rind to discover a purple flesh in the style of an orange. Its smell was obviously citrus. Nearly a blend of grapefruit, orange, and lemon rolled into one. The taste was unique and Junath considered not liking it at first. First, it was bitter and it had a licorice taste, but it matured into a very sweet lemon and orange cross. Jael tossed another one to him.

As he was eating breakfast, Junath overheard Jael speaking with Captain Regi about what they needed to do to get the word out to Palace Home and to the other passes. "Palace Home needs to be warned, but the other passes need to double up their watches to ensure there isn't a flank attack while we are focused on this pass."

"I agree Commander, but we can't afford to send too many people away from this station. It's already understaffed as it is."

"Well, what do you propose, Captain?"

There was a long pause, and then Junath spoke up, "Cal and I could help man the airship as it travels to the other passes. We're experienced in it and I wouldn't be much good at Palace Home while waiting for orders. What do ya say, Cal?"

"I just want to eat my breakfast," was Cal's terse reply, but he followed it up with, "Ah, I guess I wouldn't mind another round in the death trap you call an airship."

Looking to the captain, Jael said, "Good. Though I would prefer my brother to stick close to me, I can see the point. You take Cal, Junath, and Sergeant Byers, and the four of you fly to the other passes. Afterward, report to Palace Home. Be sure to raise Haven's banner and get rid of that Crimson one. You might get shot down otherwise."

"Yes, sir." Captain Regi saluted and turned to Cal and Junath and said, "Meet me at the airship in one hour."

After gathering supplies, Junath and Cal arrived at the airship. Jael was there waiting. "Take care, Junath. I hate to part ways again." The two brothers embraced each other. When they let go, Jael mounted his horse and said, "Safe flying, Brother." And then he and some officers galloped off west. Junath, Cal, Iris, and Lady boarded the airship.

Having a four-man crew made it a difficult task to fly the ship, but despite the skeleton crew, the airship rose off the ground and headed North along the Sanctuary Mountains. The weather was clear and cool and the flight was uneventful. The sights were gorgeous. Shortly after noon, the Captain walked up to Junath and Cal and said, "If you guys look closely off to the west, you can see the glitter of Palace Home." As Junath looked out the port side of the ship, he saw the sparkling Haven capital shining by the early afternoon sun.

Junath turned and looked at the Captain and said, "I bet it's beautiful."

"It is the most beautiful city I have ever seen, and I have been around." The Captain continued, "Well, let's get back to getting this thing up to Central Pass. We should be getting there before nightfall."

The Captain proved quite accurate. Just before sunset, they were landing the ship at the base that supported the Central Pass. The base was very similar to the one they found at the southern one. As expected, they did not have any activity at the gate, but the commander of the camp agreed it would be wise to increase the personnel on watch.

The next morning, they all boarded the airship and began to head to the Northern Pass. According to the Captain, it would be nearly a two day trip to it, and the first day was uneventful. However, about halfway into the next day, a storm suddenly appeared. "The Western Gale is early this year. We're going to have to set her down!" yelled the Captain, but as they were trying to lower the ship to land, a strong gust of wind blasted into the side of the airbags pushing the ship higher into the air. After that, it was a fight to just stay alive. The wind roared and regardless of how much the small crew fought, they were at the mercy of the wind, and it was blowing them straight into the mountains.

"Secure that line, Sergeant! Cal, try releasing some of the gas out of the balloons to get us to land!" The Captain continued barking orders, and then the downpour began.

Soaked to the bone and tossed to and fro, Junath did his best to do as he was ordered.

CRACK! A white flash and a deafening sound exploded all around them as the ship was struck by lightning. Worse yet, it burned a massive hole in the ship's forward balloon, and the ship was engulfed in flames.

"Everyone, brace for impact!"

Junath held as tightly as he could and he felt his body lift off the deck as the ship careened toward the ground. It wasn't a long fall, but the ship fiercely slammed down onto the side of the mountain. For Junath, everything went black.

18

Pain

The Sun disturbed Junath, waking him the next day. Seeing his breath in the air and beginning to shiver, Junath knew he needed to start a fire. Taking a quick survey, he saw splintered wood all around him. "Well, at least there's plenty of firewood," he said to himself. Then he tried to lift himself, but the moment he put weight on his arm he screamed in agony. Using his other arm, he managed to sit up and looked around. The ship was unrecognizable. Then as he looked towards what would have been the bow, he saw the Captain lying still on the ground. Junath hurried to Captain Regi.

"Captain! Captain Regi!" Shaking the Captain's body with his good arm he realized the Captain did not survive the crash. Then horror washed over Junath. "Cal! Cal! Iris! LADY!" Junath looked all around and could not find any of the others, and he began to panic. "CAL! Anyone!"

"Here! Over here! I'm pinned under this beam!" Cal was alive.

Junath ran towards Cal and realizing he couldn't lift the beam himself, he hunted for another board to use as a lever. When he found it, he used a stone as a fulcrum. It was a difficult task considering he could only use one arm, but he managed to pry it up enough for Cal to climb out.

"Your arm," Cal said after dusting himself off.

"I think it is broken," was Junath's reply.

"Here, let me take a look at it. Any sign of Sergeant Byers?"

"Not yet."

Cal felt on the arm and asked where it hurt and after a couple of minutes said, "Good news and bad news. Good news, it's not broken, the bad news, well, I'm going to have to hurt you to put it back into its socket." Taking Junath's arm, he tucked the elbow against the side of his body and holding Junath's arm at a 90-degree angle at the elbow, began to rotate it back while keeping the elbow tucked at the side. The pain was nearly unbearable, and Junath grimaced through the process. Then gently easing it up from the side, Cal rotated the arm forward and like a puzzle piece, the shoulder joint slipped back into place.

Junath's face eased. Relief was instant.

"Junath, sit here and rest that arm, I will see what supplies I can gather…and maybe I can find the animals." Junath noticed a solemn look on Cal's face as he said those words. Junath too feared the worse for Iris and Lady.

However, after Cal had been gone for ten or fifteen minutes, Junath felt the rush of wind as Lady came to a landing beside him. "Lady, you are a sight for sore eyes." He petted her soft head as she tucked in her wings.

A minute or two later, Cal came back with a lowered head. "I can't find her. Iris is gone."

Junath looked at Lady and vainly asked, "Can you find her?" She took flight and began circling around. After ten minutes, she swooped down, nearly colliding with Junath and Cal. The two bolted, following her direction. Running into the forest, they climbed over rocks and fallen trees. The air was crisp, but they continued on, keeping an eye on Lady as she flew in the direction of Iris' body.

Popping over a knoll, there was her body, lying still against a tree. Cal rushed toward her and kneeling, he reached out to see if she would wake. She still didn't move. Cal began to cry. Junath walked up to Cal to comfort him and as he rested his hand on the man's shoulder, Iris stirred. She was alive but hurt and weak. Cal and Junath quickly built a litter out of two boards and some of the cloth of the airship's balloons. It took both Junath and Cal to lift the wolf onto the litter, but they managed it with little complaining from Iris. Trekking back through the forest to the crash site, it took more strength than Junath expected, especially with his tender shoulder, but after nearly an hour they were back enjoying the warmth of a fire. After a quick rest, the two decided to bury Captain Regi. They tried digging a grave, but the soil was not very deep, and it was filled with large stones. They dug a shallow grave and then made a mound of stones to finish covering him.

"Cal, while you are nursing Iris, Lady and I will head out and try to hunt some dinner and look for the sergeant."

"That sounds like a plan. Iris needs some care, but I think after a day or two of rest and warmth by the fire, she should be able to travel again. And Junath, thanks for your help today. You too, Lady, I owe you both."

"Cal, you're family. It's what we do."

Cal looked at Junath with a warm grin and said, "Yeah, yeah it is."

As Junath was packing his gear, Lady flew overhead ready for the hunt. As he headed out, he heard Cal yell, "Junath, I prefer my dinner before Lady's regurgitation!"

Turning around to face Cal, Junath said, "I'll save every pellet just for you."

19

Ghost Stories

Junath and Lady hiked for a couple of hours up farther on the mountain. The smell of pine wafted in the air, and Junath enjoyed the opportunity to explore a mountain for the first time. Though they were looking for any signs of the sergeant, their search was coming up empty.

Deciding to rest on the underside of a bluff that was heavily covered in vine, Junath pulled out his flask of water and took a drink. While he was in mid-sip, a deep metallic grinding moan came from behind him. Junath slowly turned around and from behind the thick vines, he saw a bright light coming from within the mountainside. Junath quickly rose and ran with renewed energy. A few minutes later and thoroughly frightened, Junath said, "Lady, let's take one more look around for Sergeant Byers. If you don't see him, I'm ready to head back to camp."

As she did before, Lady took to the sky and began a circling pattern. This time, she came back swooping low and made a direct line northeast of their current direction. Junath went running in her direction. She had found the sergeant. He was alive but severely injured.

"Sergeant Byers!" Junath yelled.

Weakly, Sergeant Byers wheezed, "Junath, you made it…." He was interrupted by a short raspy cough. "…Did everyone make it?"

"No, Captain Regi died in the crash."

A look of sorrow swept across his face before he replied, "We lost a good officer. I have served with him for many years." After a moment of reflection, he asked Junath to help him up. When Junath got him standing, it was obvious it was going to be difficult. After about 20 steps, Sergeant Byers collapsed too weak to move further and in excruciating pain.

Looking at Lady, Junath said, "I need Cal's help." Without losing a moment, she took off in the direction of the camp.

"Here, here's some water." Junath held Sergeant Byers' head up as he gave him a drink.

"Thank you, young man. I'm feeling stronger already."

"Cal should be here soon, and once I get this fire finally lit, you'll really be feeling better.".

"You know Junath, as a kid, we were all told to be afraid of these mountains. Ghosts were said to roam them. Now it seems I will be named among them too."

"We'll fix you up, Sergeant Byers."

"Please call me Ronal."

But startled by the mentioning of ghosts, Junath asked, "Are the stories about ghosts just stories to scare children?"

"Ha ha…" again his coughing interrupted his laugh, but he continued, "Son, I would have answered yes if it weren't for last night. I heard strange things like a heavy grinding and an eerie humming. I didn't see anything, but I sure wished I didn't spend the night alone after the crash."

"Just before I met you, I heard something similar. When I turned around, I think I saw a ghost."

"Son, there's mysteries innumerable about these mountains. It would seem we have stumbled on another one. Let's hope the ghost is a kind one." Reaching with his hand he asked, "Can I have another drink of that water?" Junath handed him the flask.

For the next 20 minutes, Junath sat silent and kept thinking about the ghost in the mountain. It consumed his thoughts until Cal and Lady arrived with the litter. Junath stomped out the fire and covered the coals with dirt and then helped Cal lift Ronal onto the litter. About halfway to camp, the sergeant began coughing, and his coughing contained blood. They took a break to make sure he was fine, but the sergeant was very pale and weak.

Ronal asked in barely above a whisper, "Boys, can I ask you two a favor?"

Cal kneeled down next to him and asked, "Go ahead, soldier."

"My…my wife…if I don't make…tell her I never stopped loving her. We had a bad falling out when I left. I told her I was done…but I was a fool to leave on such a sour note. Tell her I'm sorry and give her these. She knows how valuable they are to me. They are my father's." Ronal handed Cal two medals that had long lost any ribbon that was attached to them, but in their place, a hole was bored and a small chain was threaded through them.

Cal closed Ronal's hands back over the small treasures and said, "You hold on to these, and give them to her yourself."

Again Ronal's coughing started and again it was accompanied by blood. He started grimacing and clutching his belly, and looking up at Cal, he said, "I doubt I will see the light of another day."

Junath and Cal managed to get Ronal back to camp and laid him next to the fire. Junath and Lady went out to finally get the hunt done he had set out to do earlier. It did not take long, and the two came back just before sunset with three rabbits. After cleaning and cooking them over the fire, the three men and the two animals ate their food leaving nothing wasted. Ronal and Iris ate little and were fast asleep shortly after dinner. Lady took off and perched herself in a tree as if to keep watch.

Cal poked at the fire and Junath sat with his knees tucked under his chin. Looking at Cal, Junath finally said, "I saw something today that I can't explain. I'm not sure I want to explain it."

Cal looked at Junath saying, "A tragedy like this crash is something that is hard to accept, even for a war-worn soldier."

"No, Cal, something different. I was afraid. While I was looking for Sergeant Byers, I heard and saw a ghost. Sergeant Byers heard the noise during the night. He said it was a grinding noise just like I heard too."

"A what? A ghost? There are no such things as ghosts."

"Yeah, well you didn't see what I saw. It came right up behind me. I sat down for a break just under a small rock hanging, and just behind some thick vines, I felt the rumble and the grinding, and then when I turned I saw this bright light shining through the vines. It was a ghost, I tell ya."

"Ghosts are just stories to scare kids. I've traveled all over this land and I have never seen any proof of anything like ghosts."

"Well, something's up there. I aim to go see it again tomorrow…during the daylight of course."

"I might fancy the adventure myself, just to make sure you are keeping your wits about ya." Cal then stretched himself out by the fire and said, "Now, I think I will get some sleep too. At least tonight I don't have to sleep with a wooden beam as a blanket."

Junath too laid down and using the torn balloon as a sleeping bag, he closed his eyes. Sleep eluded him while his mind dwelt on the ghost of the mountain. But eventually, he was carried off by a sound sleep.

20

Medal Metal Mettle

Junath woke before the dawn, and he quickly gathered his gear while trying to muster his courage to face the ghost of the mountain. Before he left, he gathered more firewood so Iris and Ronal could have the comfort of the fire.

When Junath returned to the camp, Cal was already up. Cal was bent over the embers from the previous fire and he was encouraging the flames to come back to life. Using some of the tinder that was around, it was not long before it was a strong fire once again. Cal went over to Sergeant Byers to tell him they were leaving when he discovered that Sergeant Byers' life had left his body.

"Junath," there was a pause in Cal voice that caught Junath's attention, and Junath looked straight at the lifeless body. "Our trip to see your ghost is going to have to wait."

Junath came over and knelt beside the man's body, and he placed his hand on his heart and said, "I'm sorry Ronal, I'm so sorry." Cal pulled Sergeant's Byers medals from his clutched fist and tucked them into his pack.

"Let's lay him to rest, Junath."

The morning was spent gathering stones from the mountainside to bury Sergeant Byers beside Captain Regi. Twin graves laid; two valiant soldiers lost. Afterward, the four survivors ate their lunch in silence.

When Junath and Cal were ready to leave, Iris again remained at the camp to continue to recover from her injuries. So, the three began the hike to make heads or tales of the ghost on the mountain.

Since he knew the exact location, the hike only took about an hour and fifteen minutes, but when they got to the bluff, there was nothing obviously out of the ordinary. The only noises they heard were the sounds of the forests and the wind blowing through the tops of the trees.

"Hmm, I was right here when the light came out from behind these roots and vines, but now nothing." Junath sat down in front of the vines to see if he could recreate the situation that brought the ghost out the last time, but again the results proved futile.

Cal reached his hand to touch the vines and said, "So the light showed through the cracks between these vines right?"

"Yeah,"

"I wonder what's behind these vines then."

Picking up on what Cal was thinking, Junath said, "I got my hatchet, let's find out."

With that Junath and Cal began hacking at the roots and vines, pulling them off with great effort. Once they got a small clearing, they discovered something beyond belief. Just behind the foliage was a solid, smooth panel made out of metal. Eager to get the metal exposed completely they worked tirelessly to finish removing the vegetation.

After an hour of hard labor, they finally found that the metal wall was about 6 feet wide and about ten feet high.

"What is it, Cal?"

"I've no idea, I have never seen anything this smooth or made out of metal that didn't rust after this long in the woods." Cal took his fist and pounded on the wall, but it sounded as solid as the mountain."It looks like it is perfectly fused into the rock around it, I don't see anything."

Junath and Cal searched and searched for anything that could help tell them what it was, and they even walked along the bluff to see if there were any other anomalies such as this, but this was the only one they could find. After half an hour of vain searching, they decided to take a break and get a bite to eat.

Sitting with their backs to the forest and facing the metal wall, they began to eat. They had not gotten one bite in when the rough grinding and deep vibrations started.

"Look Cal, it's moving!"

The metal was sliding to the right. On the left side, a bright light started shining out from behind the moving wall.

Fear was the first emotion, but after the metal disappeared into the adjacent rock, the light revealed a long hallway leading straight into the mountain.

With an astonished look on his face, Cal said, "Never in my life…"

"Do we go in?"

"I don't know Junath, I don't know what it is."

Lady, however, made the answer for them and she flew into the mountain.

"I guess that answers that," Cal said as he looked in disbelief.

Junath grinned at Cal with a wink and said, "Where's your mettle? It's not like it's a ghost."

Cal pursed his lips and replied, "Har...har...har... You should have seen the 'mettle' on your face when you thought it was a ghost." Then walking into the tunnel he added, "Well, aren't ya coming?"

21

Unknown History

Junath glided his hand down the cool smooth metallic wall. "Cal, how can this be?"

"Beats me, kid."

Junath saw a panel on the wall emanating light. He walked up to it and expected the light to be hot, but it was just as cool as the walls. They walked silently until they came to an intersection. Written on the wall was a sign with an arrow pointing to the left that said, "Utilities and Maintenance" An arrow pointed to the right saying, "Command."

Junath and Cal looked down both hallways, and Cal said, "Let's see who's running this place."

They walked again for a few minutes and came to another intersection, this time a new sign for the library pointed opposite of command.

Looking ahead Junath said, "The hallway to 'Command' has collapsed."

"I guess we had better try that library," Cal said.

At the end of the hall, there was a set of doors with a sign that said, "Library."

They stepped up to the door and with a hiss of air, the doors slid open.

"Yeah, that's not creepy."

With a grin, Junath replied, "You getting scared now?"

"Someone's gotta protect ya. We've gone this far, might as well see what's in here."

The books were old and very fragile. Junath picked one off the shelf, and the title was nearly worn off. When he opened the book, many of the pages just crumbled as if they were ash. Setting the book back on the shelf, Junath walked deeper into the library. Then he saw a table with a light shining down onto a lone book that lay open.

Junath walked up to it, and Cal was right behind him. He reached out and touched the book, but the book did not disintegrate to the touch, but it felt like thin leather. There were words written on the pages, and a small metal stylus pointed to a set of words, and Junath read them out loud saying, "But I say unto you, Love your enemies, bless them that curse you, do good to them that hate you, and pray for them which despitefully use you, and persecute you."

Cal's reply was, "Humph, that sounds like the quickest way to make a fool of yourself. It looks like that philosophy did these people a lot of good seeing that there's no one here alive."

Just as Cal stopped speaking, the light began to flicker and a woman appeared on the table before them. She was tall, poised, beautiful, and she held a copy of the book that was laying on the table.

"Greetings, I am Dr. Phillipa Maine. It is the Year of our Lord 2165. It is with great sadness I make this recording, but if you are listening to it, it means that someone has survived the war."

Cal walked around the table and waved his arms through her image, but his hand just passed through her.

The woman continued, "The world is at war, and we are all that remains to protect the greatest treasure and weapon. It is this very book that I hold and will leave on this table for those who will come after us. This book is an endangered volume, for our governments on this earth have conspired to destroy all copies and silence the voices of those who follow after the true King, Jesus of Nazareth.

"I have heard there are some who are protecting this book in other parts of the world, but in these parts, we only have three copies. We have decided to leave this one here, and use the other two to hopefully share with others willing to listen. The answer to peace on earth is found on these pages, and though I may lose my life for defending and sharing them, I know I will rise when my King comes back. This specific verse found in Matthew chapter five and verses 43 and 44 holds the key to the turmoil that has embroiled the whole globe. 'You have heard that it has been said, you shall love your neighbor, and hate your enemy. But I say unto you, love your enemies, bless them that curse you, do good to them that hate you, and pray for them which despitefully use you, and persecute you.' If only our leaders would have embraced this eternal truth, perhaps we could have avoided this genocide.

"73 years ago an asteroid crashed into New York City. Anarchy swept the country. War was really inevitable for the United States, but when the 2nd Civil War erupted, what fragments were left of the government soon dissipated into nothing. It was a matter of time before the whole world collapsed into an economic depression that shattered most of the world's governments. This catastrophe wiped out nearly three-quarters of the world's population, but the worse was yet to come.

"Carlos Montoya rules most of the Americas, Mikhail Petrov has nearly conquered Asia and Europe, and Serge Okeke has managed to unite the African Continent. All three are hostile to any religion, especially Christianity. And being set on global domination, they are proving steadfast in their cruel conquest.

"About seventeen years ago, we began to feel religious harassment ease when Carlos Montoya's chief servant converted to Christ. But our rejoicing was short-lived. The other two dictators saw this as their opportunity to strike against Montoya, thinking he was weakening. Montoya lashed out more aggressively towards us and the War began. The first missiles were launched five years ago, and our world has been in perpetual winter. Millions more are dying of starvation and yet this war continues. Christians everywhere are pleading for the Lord to come, and we are trying to trust in His timing. But I groan in my spirit, ready to see Him on the clouds.

"However, it soon became apparent that we are all that remains of Christianity here in this region. We hear of others, but communication is limited. Our elders decided to preserve our library and a copy of the Bible on parchment. We were blessed to make three. If you found this book and this library, please treasure these keepsakes knowing that those who hoarded these most likely have perished in the flames of war. But it is with hope, we leave this greatest of all treasures that maybe if this world continues, mankind will find its way again to serve God. Take this Bible, read it, believe it, live it, and share it. May God be with us all."

After she said those words, Dr. Phillipa Maine's image disappeared with a flicker. Junath slowly closed the book and started to put it into his pack.

"Personally, I would leave it."

"I don't know, Cal, perhaps there is something in this book that will help us against the Crimson Army."

"It didn't help them against those three dictators, why would it help us? Just let it be."

"No, I am going to see what it says. What could it possibly hurt?" With that Junath secured the book in his pack.

"Suit yourself. Come, let's get back to camp and get some rest. This day has been weird enough."

22

Another Airship

Very little discussion took place that evening and the next morning. But since Iris was acting more herself, the party set out on a two day hike for the Northern Pass. As they approached the village near the gate, they saw an airship with Crimson markings. Walking around the ship were Crimson soldiers clothed in their black uniforms. As the sky began to grow dim with the coming of night, Cal and Junath crept up to the camp to try to eavesdrop on the soldiers to learn what their plans were.

"Wish I were at the southern border where the real fighting will be," one soldier said as he kneeled by the fire.

"I don't know, we have a chance to cripple Haven for the army is at the Southern Pass. Plus, we get to prove ourselves before General Kein." The other soldier replied as he began to roast a small animal over the fire.

"I guess you're right, it would be a great opportunity for promotion, but sitting here babysitting some prisoners isn't really what I was promised."

"We were recruited to do what we were told to do, and we had best learn to be content with it."

"Attention!"

Both soldiers stood upright, looked forward, and held their arms to their sides. Junath looked at the officer who approached; it was Finister Kein. Junath's heart sank deeper and the cut on his face ached.

Walking up to the soldiers Kein said, "Listen up, you and the other enlisted are to remain here and execute these prisoners. In ten minutes, I will take the Jonpetis and we will begin our flight to Palace Home. There we will infiltrate and assassinate the Chancellor. If all goes as planned we will arrive back here in three days' time. I expect this camp to be cleared, these prisoners strung up, and everyone ready for an immediate flight back to the army at the Southern Pass. Am I understood?"

Both men gave a hearty, "Yes, Sir!"

"Good," was his only reply and Finister Kein turned and left.

Cal looked at Junath and said, "We need to get on that ship and try to stop them."

"I'm ready if you are I guess. I need to send a message to my brother. He's not expecting an attack from the north." As Junath got out some paper to write the note on, his face became inquisitive. "What are the Jonpetis?"

"The 'Pets' as I call 'em are elite Crimson soldiers. They work as spies, saboteurs, and they say they can scale a wall just like a lizard. I've seen a couple, but they usually stay out of sight. They are very dangerous, and if they are going to be on that ship, we had best keep our eyes open extra wide." After a moment, Cal continued, "Hey listen, do you see those large trees just beyond the ship?"

"Yes."

"Once you get that message off, meet me and Iris there as soon as possible."

"Ok, but what are you planning?"

"Improvising really, just get to it, our time is short." Cal and Iris darted off into the woods.

Junath began to scratch a message. Afterward, he rolled it around Lady's leg and tied it on.

"Lady, find my brother and give him this warning about the Chancellor's life. Go, hurry!" Understanding her mission, Lady was off to find Jael.

Junath kept hidden in the shadows and made his way to the trees on the other side of the Crimson Camp. He wasn't there but a minute before he heard Finister Kein bark out, "Set Sail!"

Junath looked frantically around for Cal but did not see him or Iris. "Come on, Cal," Junath whispered, "Don't let me get on there by myself."

After another moment, the airship began to slowly move. Junath gave another quick look and still didn't see Cal. "Great…" he said and then made a run for the ship. Grabbing hold of a net hanging on the side, Junath was able to climb up. He looked through a port window to see if it was clear. When he was about to climb through, he heard the sound of someone coming up behind him. He turned back to see Iris and Cal making their way to catch up with him. Hooking his legs in the net, he hung down and reached to grab Iris, but he was a little too high.

Junath curled back up and climbed a little further down the net, and hung upside down again. This time Cal had managed to grab Iris and hoisted her up to Junath. Being a wolf, Iris was not exactly a light pup, and Junath struggled to get her to the port window. By the time he got her to the window, Cal had climbed up and was able to assist him.

Finally, all three sat inside the room and began to catch their breaths. Junath, panting, looked over at Cal and said through a heavy whisper, "Is that what you call improvising nowadays?"

"I cut it kinda close, didn't I?"

"What were you doing anyway?"

"Well," Cal gave a small pause and with a smirk said, "I gave the prisoners a fighting chance by cutting their bonds and telling them where the temporary armory was. Did you get your message off?"

"Yes, I did. What's your plan when we get to Palace Home?"

"I'll figure it out when we get there."

With a smile, Junath looked at Cal and replied, "Still improvising, uh?" Cal only grinned back.

Cal looked around at his surroundings and with a sigh said, "Great, another airship."

23

Palace Home

Junath spent all of his free time reading the book he got from the library. He was having difficulty making much sense of it and was bouncing from page to page. But after a while, he decided to read about the man Jesus, beginning from the page that Dr. Maine suggested in her message. Cal continued to scoff at the notion that the book was of any true value.

During the night after two uncomfortable days of travel, Junath felt the airship land. Cal looked at Junath and lifted his finger to keep quiet. He slipped out the port window to get some intel on where they were and the progress of the Crimson mission. During the fifteen-minute wait, Junath gathered all their belongings ready to evacuate the ship when Cal returned. It was not long after Junath finished packing that Cal peeped back through the window.

"Whatcha find, Cal?"

"We've landed about ten miles northeast of Palace Home, and they are waiting until tomorrow night to make their move so they can have the new moon for cover. Come on, let's get going before they set up their camp."

Junath, Cal, and Iris were off quickly and deep into the woods before the Crimsons had a chance to realize they were not alone in the airship. After a three hour hike, they came up to the clearing that led to Palace Home. The sun had risen well above the horizon.

"If Lady made it here, they will be on high alert."

"Lady made it," Junath replied confidently.

It was not long before there was a garrison of soldiers riding horseback meeting them on the road.

The lead horseman approached, saying, "Hail, what business have two wanderers and a wolf at Palace Home? These are perilous times, and we are short on hospitality."

"Sir, we are friends of Jael Symp. This is his brother Junath Symp. Jael gave us orders to warn the central and northern passes, but we were late for the North. Time is of the essence."

The soldier looked at Cal then Junath, then said, "Hmm, his features do resemble Jael's. Presently, Jael is in the castle. He will be able to verify the truth of your statements." Looking over to a couple of the other soldiers, he continued, "Blindy, Colve, make room for these two to ride."

Two men said, "Aye, sir," and they reached down and each took one and pulled him onto the back of his respective horse.

The lead horseman again took the lead and hurried back to the gate of the palace. As they approached, the oak doors creaked open, and they entered.

The site of the market place was very somber. It was as if everyone knew that death could be knocking on their doors soon, but still, business continued. Traders made agreements, and barterers were negotiating. The sounds of chickens, pigs, and cows were heard over the constant sound of human voices mingled with clinging coin.

As the soldiers passed through the gate, it rattled closed. The cavalry unit continued down the path toward the palace. It took a good twenty minutes to navigate the streets, houses, and shops to get to the proper Keep.

The Keep was a beautiful white stone castle with blue terracotta tiles for the roofs. Five towers rose above a center building, and the wall enclosing the keep was thirty feet thick.

As they approached the gate of the keep, the guards asked the soldiers about the nature of their business. The lead horseman replied, "We've picked up these travelers just outside the city, and they have claimed to be with Commander Symp. If he could be so kind as to verify these two men and a wolf, then our job will be done."

"We will track him down as soon as possible; it's a madhouse in here as

you well know."

"Indeed, I do, but please do make haste."

The guard turned to the squire next to him and whispered some order, and the young man was off. After thirty minutes, the squire's quest was successful, and Junath saw Lady fly over the wall, and she landed on his arm. Junath then looked up and saw Jael smiling ear to ear at the current company before him.

"Captain, these men are indeed with me. See, the owl recognizes my blood." Turning to the guards in the gatehouse, he said, "Lower the bridge and let them in, I am eager to hear more of this looming attack."

Inside, Jael led them to the conference room where the Chancellor and a number of high officials sat. They were being served breakfast. Places were made for Junath and Cal, and even food was given to Iris, and she was quite content.

Guiding Junath and Cal to the table, Jael introduced them to the Chancellor, "Chancellor Manaen, this is my brother Junath, and his mentor Cal."

The Chancellor stood and reached his hand out, shaking Junath's first and then turned to Cal and asked as he shook his hand, "Where are you from, Ranger?"

"Chancellor, I am from Tuckshire. I have been a wanderer ever since Shorne Forte destroyed my home and killed my family."

"I am sorry to hear about that, but come and join me at my table. Maybe you can aid us, so we don't suffer the same loss as you.

"Thank you, sir. I serve to end the Crimson rise."

"Good, good," replied Chancellor Manaen. Then he continued, "Gentlemen, let's have a seat."

Chancellor Manaen was a respectable middle-aged man. His hair was deeply grayed, but his face still kept a youthful appearance. However, of all his facial features, it was his brilliant green eyes that Junath would never forget. His manner of dress was strikingly not as militarized as was his officers at the table, but it still made known his station in Haven.

Sitting down, they all ate their food solemnly, knowing that the meal prefaced a somber reality for the nation. They finished quickly and began right away with preparations for the looming attack.

Chancellor Manaen began the dialogue. "Gentleman, early yesterday Jael received word," looking over at Junath, he continued, "from a rather strange source, that revealed that the Northern Pass has fallen, and an attack on Palace Home is imminent. Yesterday, we took an inventory of our supplies, including personnel. Unfortunately, we have our bulk force marching to the Southern Pass as we speak. Had we not been warned, we too would have been leaving today in that march, but fate has us here making our stand.

"I must tell you, we are not prepared for an attack, and our intel is very scant." Looking back to Cal and Junath, he said, "Unless you two have any further information."

Cal spoke up and said, "Yes sir, I would expect a covert attack by a unit of 'Pets" to happen tonight. The airship that we snuck aboard on was only staffed by Jonpetis. I only could count about forty, but I would suspect more."

Jael, a little stunned, said, "You guys stowed away on a Crimson Airship full of Jonpetis and didn't get caught? You two are beyond daring. You border insane!"

"I've argued that about myself for years," Cal said, and then continuing, he added, "The only other soldier was Finister Kein."

The room's occupants sank farther into their chairs.

"By the sound of the quietness, I take it you all are familiar with Kein's reputation?"

Chancellor Manaen said, "Unfortunately, we are, but please continue. Where is this airship?"

Cal said, "It is ten miles northeast of here. They plan to attack tonight during the new moon."

Looking down at the table, Chancellor Manaen said, "Then we have come to our moment. Tonight's the night."

After a pause, he looked at all the men in the room, and grief was on his face, but then it grew stern and controlled. After a short pause, he said, "Men tonight will be a hard night, we all must be at our best. There is very little we can do now that we haven't already done. Everyone take a little time to love your families. We'll report back here at mid-afternoon to finalize our preparations."

At that moment, a servant came in walking toward the Chancellor. When he approached the Chancellor, he whispered in his ear. The Chancellor nodded and said, "Send her in, please."

A moment after the servant left, a young woman entered the room. She had an elegant grace about her, and her rich, thick auburn hair adorned her head in a beautiful braid, and her eyes were as piercing green as her father's. Junath was stunned and, for a moment, forgot he was in the company of Generals and the Chancellor until a stiff elbow from Cal pulled him from his stupor. The elbowing drew the woman's attention, and as she looked straight into the eyes of Junath, his face flushed red as the beets he harvested on his farm. He looked at Jael, who was staring at him with a grin that nearly turned into laughter.

The woman moved toward the Chancellor and spoke to him with urgency. A pursed frown appeared on the Chancellor's face, and he took the young woman's hand and gently patted it, saying, "I will be right there." Looking at the men at the table, he said, "It would seem my orders for the family must include my own. My daughter tells me my mother has taken a turn for the worse. If she survives until evening, then we'll be graced with a few hours beyond our hopes. Again, go and report back here at mid-afternoon. You're dismissed."

Upon the dismissal, Chancellor Manaen stood up and left with his daughter. Junath kept his gaze on the beautiful young woman leaving.

Leaning over Junath's shoulder Jael said, "Her name is Ithleah, and yes, she is your age."

"Jael, I've never seen a girl as beautiful as her."

"Well, that is because you haven't met Isabella and Tirzah. Come, you have family to meet." Grabbing his shoulders, he pushed Junath toward the doors.

"You're welcome too, Cal," Jael said, "Isabella is always fixing something to eat."

"I guess I'll come on then since there'll be food involved."

24

Family

Led by Jael, the three entered through a door in the west wing of the castle. The moment Jael walked through, a little voice called out excitedly, "Daddy home!"

A little girl about two years of age ran up and Jael snatched her up into his arms, turning to Junath with a huge smile on his face. He said, "Junny, meet your niece Tirzah." The sandy-blonde-haired little girl gave a quick look at Junath and then buried her face on her daddy's shoulder.

"Come on, Tirzah, I know you're not shy," but she clung tighter.

"Jael? You're home?" A woman called from another room just before she came around the corner.

"Bell, come quick, I have someone I want you to meet."

Isabella came into the room. She was a youthful-looking beautiful woman in her early thirties with dark hair, nearly black, and she had dark brown eyes.

"I bet you're Junath," she said as she approached.

"I am," Junath suddenly grew anxious as he looked upon the woman who was the daughter of his enemy. She was the reason for Seren's death, but he shook the negative thoughts away. He reached his hand out but she gave him a hug.

She stepped back, and with a joyful smile, she said, "Jael couldn't stop talking about how he found his brother, and he was getting kinda worried that it was taking you guys so long get here. But here you are."

"And Bell, this other fella is Cal Whist. He's the one who's taken Junath under his wing to train him." Jael motioned toward Cal who was standing by the wall. "Come on everyone, let's have a seat."

They all sat down on the couches except for Isabella. She went into the pantry and came back with some freshly squeezed cornamen juice, crackers, and sliced white cheese. Being full, Junath didn't eat much of the cheese and crackers, but he did enjoy the juice.

Still having to hold onto Tirzah, Jael asked, "So tell me what happened after we separated, and where are Captain Regi and Sergeant Brown?"

Junath lowered his head and replied, "Both are dead. Captain Regi called it a Western Gale and the airship crashed into the mountains."

Cal also added, "Captain Regi was dead by the time Junath and I came around, and we found Ronal later, but he died through the next night. We nearly lost Iris too, but after a few days rest she's as ornery as ever."

Jael said, "They were two of the best, and they will be sorely missed." He then asked, "Where are Iris and Lady anyways?"

"Junath and I kept them outside. I ought to be checking on them soon."

Tirzah crawled out of her daddy's lap and started to munch on a cracker in one hand and a piece of cheese in the other. Junath reached over and said hello. She turned and buried her face into the couch beside her father. Isabella came behind Junath and handed him a small candy and said, "Here, bribe her with this."

Grabbing the candy he said, "Tirzah, look what I have." She turned and saw the candy and started for it, but then hesitated. Junath continued, "It's ok little girl, you can have it, but you have to smack my hand." He reached his hand out flat and she raised her hand and smacked palm against palm.

"Here you go." He handed her the candy and she ate it up with cheese and cracker still in her mouth. "Can I hold ya?" Junath asked.

She came nervously up to him but allowed him to pick her up. Junath was then overwhelmed by the emotion he had for this little kid. This was his niece, his own flesh and blood.

Tears began to well up in Jael's eyes when he said, "You know, I was your age when I left, and you were about a year older than Tirzah. It broke my heart to leave you. You couldn't sleep by yourself and I was the one you always chose. I'm so sorry I left. I didn't understand then what I was doing to you, but now that I have a little one, I grieve that I was not there while you grew up and needed me. I know Dad did well, but I am your brother. I would have been the second most influence, if not the first, in your life. I blew it…"

Junath set Tirzah down on the floor and standing, he embraced Jael. They sobbed on each other's shoulders and Jael said, "Never again will I abandon you or anyone that I love."

"Nor will I. I forgive you, and I am sorry for being so angry before."

Cal stood and said, "Well, with this homecoming and bromance spewing, I think I will take my leave and check on Iris."

Stepping away from Jael, Junath added, " I think I will join you to check on Lady." Then he looked at Jael and said, "When I get back, I need to tell you what we found on that mountain. It's like nothing I've ever seen."

"You didn't see the ghosts of the mountains, did you?" Jael said with a chuckle.

"Uh, as a matter of fact, yes, yes we did, and I need to tell you about it. But let me tell you when I get back."

"Really, the ghosts are just old wives' tales. Hey, let me lead you two out. I need to check on the Chancellor's mother anyway." Jael looked at Isabella and said, "Mrs. Manaen has gotten worse. I will only be a few minutes. Then I'll be back."

"That's fine, Tirzah and I'll be here." She leaned and gave Jael a kiss, and Jael knelt down and gave Tirzah a hug. The three then left the suite and walked down the hall.

"So what did you find in the mountain?"

"A facility of some sort, that is beyond any technology we possess. Lights that were bright, but had no heat. And in the library, we saw a ghost. If that is what you want to call it. It seems to be a relic of the past, but she spoke and told us the history of her time," Junath said.

"What's your take, Cal?"

"I could wave my hand through her. She did not respond to us, but she spoke like she lived in a very different time. The place was deep inside the mountain. The structure was made by someone far more skillful than any one of our day could replicate. Of all my wanderings, I have never seen anything of this nature. In fact, the technology was even more advanced and elaborate than the gate at the Southern Pass."

"Jael, have you ever seen or heard of anything like this before?"

"No, no I haven't. What all did she tell you?"

"She spoke of a time when her world was being destroyed and that three dictators were conquering the world."

"This must have been a long time ago because there are no signs of any such society. Yes, there is not much known historically more than a thousand years ago. Rumors are that we were more advanced, but no proof other than a few scant mentions in a couple of books, but we just passed them off as myth. I guess they were true. Did you find anything else?"

Junath pulled his pack around and pulled out the book Dr. Maine had told him to take. "She said this book contains the answer to peace."

Cal interjected, "Yeah, I seriously doubt it, peace certainly didn't come to her and her people."

"Hmm, what does this book say?" Jael asked.

"I have read just portions and it talks about a man who lived long ago, possibly thousands of years before Dr. Maine. This man was named Jesus and people called him Christ. I am not sure what Christ means, but he was suppose to be some kind of king sent to save his people. However, he too died by the hands of his own people and the nation that was ruling over them. That nation sounds very similar to the Crimsons. Brutal and violent."

"So this savior couldn't even save himself?" Cal said

"But here is where the story gets interesting. Jesus was only dead for three days, and he rose from the grave. I am still unsure of what to make of this story, but it is certainly intriguing. But here is the crazy part. This Jesus expects his followers to love their enemies."

"That's a tall order. This sounds silly," Jael said as they reached the door leading out of the building.

Iris ran right up to Cal and Lady lighted on Junath's arm. Junath, following up Jael's comment said, "I'm not sure yet what to make of it. I haven't read of any special weapon that could bring peace, and I really don't see how 'love' can have any effect like that."

"Speaking of 'love,'" Cal said, "You certainly were mesmerized by the Chancellor's daughter this morning."

Blushing, Junath replied, "Oh you're imagining things."

"Sure he is," Jael said with a chuckle, "but on our way back to our quarters, we will stop by and check on the Chancellor's mother. It'll also give you a chance to meet Ithleah." Junath's blush deepened.

After a few minutes, Jael and Junath headed back inside. Cal decided to remain outside and explore Palace Home to find Ronal's home before the conference. When they approached the Chancellor's quarters, they saw several in mourning and Junath knew that the Chancellor's mother did not survive.

"Chancellor Manaen, my deepest sympathies on this tragic hour," Jael said embracing the Chancellor.

"Thank you, my good friend, your love means a lot."

The Chancellor looked at Junath and said, "Young man, I'm sorry that so much has befallen you, but you seem to have the aptitude of an officer to have survived your trek. When this all settles down, you must tell me of your adventure."

"Yes sir, and I am also very sorry for your loss," Junath said.

"That is very kind of you, but we were prepared for this. Mother had been ill for weeks, and we are surprised she lasted this long."

Before Junath could offer a reply, Ithleah walked toward the small group.

Chancellor Manaen spoke, "Junath, meet my daughter Ithleah, I suppose you two are around the same age."

Ithleah reached her hand out toward Junath and he took it in his hand. He gave a courteous bow.

"I'm sorry about your grandmother," Junath said releasing her hand.

"She suffered greatly this past week, but she's at peace. I'm told you had to watch your father die. I couldn't begin to know the pain you feel from your loss." Ithleah said empathetically.

"Thank you, I miss him every day. The saddest part is that now I can't learn more about him and apparently, there was much about him that he kept secret. But the pain of the loss grows more bearable each day, you will heal. Treasure the memories you had with her."

Chancellor Manaen spoke up, "Wisdom beyond your years, Junath. Many of your age fail to grasp the importance of those memories. Especially the opportunities to make them while you have the chance. Never forget that, young man." Looking around he added, "Please excuse me while I meet with my other guests."

Jael excused the Chancellor with a bow and Junath followed his lead, bowing gracefully.

"I too must leave," said Ithleah, "Jael, take care of my father tonight. I don't think I could bear the weight of losing Grandma and him both in one day."

"I will serve with vigilance," Jael said, giving a bow.

Looking over at Junath she said, "It was good to meet the one I have heard many tales about, and I look forward to getting to know you better. Thank you both for coming by."

Both Jael and Junath said, "Good-by."

When she had left, Jael grabbed Junath's shoulder and said, "Come, let's go rest while we have a few hours left before the conference."

25

The Attack

Junath spent his time playing with Tirzah, who grew very comfortable with him. She would sit on his lap, grab his face, and make faces at him, or she would hide and then jump on Junath. Jael finally stood up and said, "Come on, Junny, let's go."

They headed to the meeting room where everyone was starting to gather. Cal, the Chancellor, and several others were already huddled around the table with a map stretched across it. As Junath approached, he noticed it was a map of Palace Home next to a map of the palace itself.

"The bulk of our army should be halfway to Southern Pass," An officer said, "But we still have a portion of our cavalry quartered in the city. We can place them at these key places on the wall." He pointed to seven places on the map.

The Chancellor looked up and seeing Jael and Junath enter, waved them to approach. Looking at the others at the table he continued, "My guard, with Jael at point, will keep me secured in the Lock Room. It's hidden, and few know of it, but I can still monitor the attack."

Jael spoke up, "Chancellor, I would recommend that we use a decoy and take you somewhere that no one would expect. I'm thinking even outside of the city. We could take the servant's tunnels to the gardens outside the walls. No one would see us leave. A small number can keep quiet."

"Jael, I appreciate this, but I was elected to lead and not cower away. I don't even like being in the Lock Room, much less leaving the city when it is under attack. No, I will take my chances here with you and the guard by my side."

"Understood Sir."

Another officer spoke up, "And we will need to place a few soldiers at key places here at the Palace itself."

"Take six of my guard and place them where you see fit, Commander Haws."

Cal said, "I'm a tracker. Junath and I can scour the perimeter and try to gather intel on their approach. Since Junath can send messages to Jael by Lady, we can keep you all informed with what we find."

"That's a great idea," Chancellor Manaen said, "Jael, what are your thoughts on that."

"Sir, it is a solid strategy, but I would petition you to not let my brother participate tonight…"

Junath interrupted, "Wait. What? No, I want to help!"

Jael continued, "I have lost my father, and I am not ready to put my brother in that type of danger again."

"I will be fine, don't do this," again Junath protested.

The chancellor let out a sigh with a soft hum.

"Please, sir, grant me this desire."

"We are short-handed tonight and could use every available person, but you have suffered greatly." And with another sigh, he added, "I will grant you your wish."

Junath stormed out of the room. Jael chased him and said, "Junny, wait."

"I've come all this way without you, and I can certainly do this tonight. Why do you choose now to be my babysitter?"

"I know, I know you are very capable, but I can't bear the thought of losing you. Can't you understand that?"

Junath stared at the floor, and still angry about the situation, he pursed his lips.

"Junath, I don't want to risk anything happening to you. Besides, there is no one I trust more right now to protect Isabella and Tirzah than you. Would you do that for me?"

Giving a sigh of capitulation, Junath said, "Yeah, I can do that, but you owe me."

Jael embraced his brother and said, "There's no doubt about that. Come there's still more to discuss."

The meeting continued for a couple more hours. Figuring out weak points in the city walls, expecting the possibility of a siege, and taking inventory, they weighed all the pros and cons of each strategy. Finally in agreement, the officers left the room to brief their soldiers of the plan. Jael and his team took the Chancellor to the Lock Room, and Junath sauntered back to Isabella and Tirzah, still not too happy about his assignment.

Stepping into the apartment, Junath set his belongings on the floor near the door. Tirzah was taking a nap, and Isabella poured him a glass to drink.

In the kitchen, Isabella said, "I told him you weren't going to be happy coming back here tonight."

"Guess he talked to you about it." Junath sat down on the couch.

Bringing him his drink she said, "He did, and I am grateful that you came back. Gives us time to get to know one another, and Tirzah will be very happy when she wakes up too."

Afternoon faded into evening and after some time, Junath was wondering if the attack was actually going to happen. A courier came to report all sentries clear. Junath was uneasy about it and wished, even more, he was out there with Cal and Iris. He got up and paced around, and Tirzah took the opportunity to sit on his foot and go for a ride. Junath played the part of a monster with a dragging foot and Tirzah loved it. He reached down and picked her up and began to swing her around. She squealed with delight.

Then there was a knock at the door. Isabella walked to the door to see who it was and it was a servant who came regularly. "Jackie, come in."

But Jackie was not alone. As he walked in, five black-clad soldiers walked in with him bearing the Crimson emblem, and then in walked Finister Kein.

26

The Chase

Isabella made a dash for Tirzah, but Finister grabbed her before she could move five feet. He gave her to one of his soldiers. Tirzah cried for her mother, and Junath weaponless, fought with his fists, making his way to his gear by the door. He made a strong effort and managed to bloody a nose in the fight, but he too was caught.

The servant looked over at Isabella and said, "I'm sorry, my lady, but they have captured my family and said they were going to kill them if I didn't lead them here." Then he looked at Finister and said, "Please let me go to my family."

Without looking at the servant, Finister said, "I lied."

"What! No, no, no...." Finister pierced the servant with his sword.

Finister gave orders to leave. Junath and Tirzah were tossed to a corner of the room. Junath picked up a sobbing Tirzah and tried to comfort her. Isabella started kicking, trying to get loose, but to no avail.

Finister walked over to Isabella and caressed her face and said, "You'll be my ticket to the throne."

Finister looked at his soldiers and said, "Let's get out of here." Looking at the soldier closest to Junath, he said, "They better be dead by the time you catch up with us." The soldier's only reply was a coarse, "Yes, sir," and he drew his sword.

As the men left carrying Isabella, the single soldier turned towards

Junath. Junath continued to stare into the eyes of the Jonpetis staying between him and his gear. Earlier in the evening, Isabella had set some snacks on the table, and as the Jonpetis circled the table and couch, he reached down to try a selection of the hors d' oeuvres. Helping himself to a handful of nuts, his regret was nearly immediate, for he began to choke.

It took a moment for Junath to realize what was happening since it happened so fast and he was more occupied with trying to get to his bag and gear by the door. When it dawned on Junath what was happening, his first thought was to grab his sword and run the man through before he recovered. On his knees, grasping at his throat, the man looked up at Junath knowing now his life was over, and the reality humbled him. Junath saw the man and remembered the passage that he read in the Book that said, "Love your enemies." It flooded his mind. Junath took a leap of faith and instead of running to get his sword, he lunged at the man and with a double fist clubbed him square in the back. The Jonpetis was thrown forward and landed on the edge of the table causing the nut to dislodge. He collapsed onto the floor grabbing his stomach but breathing. Junath helped the man onto the couch.

In a whisper, he said, "Why did you help me?"

"It is time for a new strategy. I heard that the secret to peace was love, and I had to try it out to see." The bewilderment of the scene overwhelmed the Jonpetis. He sat down to take it all in.

Coming to his senses, he looked at Junath and said, "If you plan to save the woman, you need to hurry."

Junath grabbed Tirzah and his gear and ran out the door. He searched frantically calling for Jael, and finally, Jael appeared around the corner running towards him. "Junath, what are you doing out, what's wrong?" Looking at Tirzah he continued, "Where's Bella?"

"Finister got her."

"What are you saying?"

"Finister has kidnapped Isabella and is heading toward Qunereel as we speak. Here take Tirzah, she needs you more than ever and there is a Jonpetis in your apartment. Have mercy on him, he let us go." Handing Tirzah to Jael, who, with a look of bewilderment on his face, watched Junath as he sprinted down the hall, negotiating the corridors until he was out of the castle.

Lady approached him the moment she saw him leave. "Fly to Cal and lead him to the Crimson ship, hurry, we don't have much time." The white owl gathered her momentum and was gone to find Cal and Iris. Junath continued to sprint to the city gates.

Reaching the gate, the guards ordered, "Halt!"

"Let me out, I have to hurry!"

"No one is allowed to enter or leave, and that includes you," said one soldier.

"They got Isabella, and if I don't hurry, they'll escape."

With a skeptical look, the other guard said, "Who has taken the lady?"

"The Crimsons!"

"There's no way that is possible, we have sentries posted all along the perimeter."

Frustrated, Junath said, "Well apparently there were some holes. Or worse, I guess someone's dead. Now can I pass?"

"Until we are told differently, our orders are the same. No one in. No one out."

"Fine, I'll find another way out," and Junath began to search for another option. Other paths up the wall and other gates had sentries with the same order. Tired of the dead ends, he had an idea. Grabbing a long pole, he ran towards a part of the wall and jammed the pole into the ground. Using the momentum, he vaulted himself into the air and nearly came short of the wall, but managed to grab the ledge and pulled himself on top.

"Halt, don't go any further!" A guard saw Junath and started to run toward him.

With no choice, Junath saw a nearby tree and made a leap for it. He managed to grab the limbs, but they were small and flexible and they bowed down with his weight until they snapped. Junath landed on his back. The wind was taken out of his lungs. Moments later the air returned, and Junath got back onto his feet and ignoring the guard's command to return, he headed toward the Crimson airship.

Maxing out his lung capacity, Junath finally made it to the airship, and the ship was making its preparations to leave. Jonpetis were everywhere cutting lines and obeying orders from Finister who was at the helm. Sneaking around behind the bushes, Junath searched for an opening to get aboard and find Isabella. Moments later, he heard a large number of horses galloping in the distance. Junath thought to himself, "Jael must be coming," Finister heard it too and barked, "Hurry, we have to leave now!"

When the soldiers were boarding the ship, he took his opportunity to climb into the hole as he did when he first stowed away with Cal. There were many soldiers walking the decks. He first went to the brig to see if Isabella was there. She wasn't.

Junath whispered, "He must have her in his quarters."

As he was searching for the room, he came across a window and saw they were already quite high, how could he save her now? Then out of nowhere, he felt a painful blow to his head, his vision grew blurry, and everything went black. Hours later he awoke in the brig, alone and caught.

27

Shorn Forte

Junath sat alone in the dark waiting for his death by the hand of Finister. But interestingly that never happened. When Finister did arrive it was several days later, and he walked up to the cell and said, "Tomorrow we'll be in Rath Qun, and I thoroughly hope Lord Forte will give me the pleasure of skewering you in front of Jael." And lowering his voice to just above a harsh whisper, he added, "I revel seeing the countenances of men collapse just before I end their pathetic lives."

"You'll lose. This anger and bitterness you posses will never be satisfied even if you have your way. Why do you hate my brother anyway?"

"Your brother stole everything from me. I was the one set to be top of the class. I was the one that was to marry Isabella. I was the one that was to have won the favor of Shorne Forte, but your brother took it all. He managed to only make himself the center of attention, but that favor is gone, and I have won. Besides, it quenches my thirst to sap a body's life, how much more true for those who have crossed me."

Looking up at Finister, Junath said, "Not a very good thirst quencher if you must keep doing it."

"We'll see when I watch Jael's horror as he watches you suffer the cold steel of my sword." Finister walked away leaving Junath again alone.

The next day, Junath felt the airship descend and when it lighted on the ground, there was an obvious sudden stop. Minutes later, soldiers dressed in the traditional Crimson uniform took Junath from the ship's brig and placed a black hood over his face.

As Junath was led through the streets of Rath Qun, the darkness of the hood could not conceal the putrid smell of rotting corpses. Even the sounds of the people shuffling their feet and the lack of enthusiasm in their voices spoke volumes of the state of the capital city of Qunereel. But after a number of minutes, Junath felt the ground beneath him turn to wood as he heard the sound of a draw bridge beneath him. And within a moment, he heard the portcullis open and he was lead into the upper city of Qunereel.

The moment Junath walked into the upper city he was able to take a deep breath of fresh air. It was clean, vibrant, and the market sounded alive. Junath heard crowds cheering as they mocked the prisoners with levity. Then with a creaking of a heavy iron door, Junath felt the sun disappear and he was lead into the palace.

"Is this him? Is this the boy?" His voice was deep and rich, and when he spoke there was a beautiful rhythm to it. Without a doubt, Junath knew he was in the presence of Shorn Forte.

Fear washed over him, and he felt a nervous twist inside his gut. He heard slow steps begin to walk towards him. The black hood was ripped off his head and Shorn grabbed a hand full of Junath's hair, forcing Junath to stare directly into the face of his enemy. His beard was close and kempt as was his hair. His features were strong, chiseled, and the grey patches in his beard and temples gave Shorn a very distinguished appearance, but his eyes were empty and only bitterness existed.

"So, you're the brother of Jael. How does it feel to be beaten?"

Junath's simple reply was, "We'll have to see about that."

"Your arrogance mirrors your brother's. He too shall fall just as your father the 'great warrior' Seren did."

At the mention of his father, Junath boiled with anger and lunged at Shorn, but Shorn's grip was ironclad, and Junath just appeared as a rag doll. Jerking his head back, Shorn looked hard into Junath's eyes, "To fight against me is vanity. You will do well to remember that, boy." Looking at the soldiers, he commanded, "Take him to the dungeon. Bring me my daughter."

As Junath was being led out of the room, he looked back and saw more soldiers bringing in Isabella. As Shorn walked up to her, Junath noticed a gentleness wash over Shorn. He lifted his hand to caress her face, but she reeled away from his touch. The gentleness Shorn displayed dissipated as a vapor, and he raised his hand and struck her across the face. Then the doors to the throne room were closed, and Junath was now in the corridor leading to the dungeons.

28

The Book

As Junath sat in the cold damp sewer of a pit called the dungeon, he wondered how he was ever going to get out of it. There was only a small hole that allowed drainage so the sewage didn't flood back into the palace, and climbing out was not an option since the walls were slick, not to mention no foot or handholds to speak of. The only way in or out was by a ladder that was dropped down into the hole. No bed, no chair, and he had to catch his food as it was tossed down to him. The dungeon was a place of misery.

After two days, a ladder was lowered down into the pit, and Junath heard the command of a guard, "Come." He climbed the steps and he was thrilled to fill his nostrils with fresh air as he left the opening of the pit. "Lord Forte has requested your audience."

Junath was led to a bath and made to wash. The sentry then gave him fresh clothes to wear and led him to the throne room. When Junath entered, Shorn Forte set crooked with one leg draped over an arm of the throne. His hand supported his head as he sat there with his eyes closed, but apparently he was aware of everything around him. Without opening his eyes or moving a muscle he said, "Leave the boy here before me, and I will call you when I am finished with him."

After the sentry was gone, and it was just Shorn and Junath alone in the throne room, he reached beside him and pulled the book Junath found in the Sanctuary Mountains. "Rumor is that this book holds a powerful secret capable of conquering nations."

Looking at the book Junath said, "That's what I'm told."

Shorn held the book out towards Junath and said, "Then begin reading it to me. I am sending Finister first thing in the morning to take command of the war against Haven, and I want every advantage."

"What if I refuse?"

"Then I'll throw you back into the dungeon."

"I'd rather die in that dungeon than give you an advantage over this war. "

Shorn swung his body around rising out of the throne, and walked over to Junath. Grabbing him by the collar, he lifted Junath to his eye level and asked, "Tell me, boy, how do you feel about my daughter Isabella?"

The question caught Junath off guard, but he was able to reply, saying, "She's my brother's wife."

"I asked how do you feel about her." His tone was harder.

"I guess I love her as my sister, which is more than what you can say." Junath kept his gaze into Shorn's eyes.

Shorn's eyes narrowed and he began to grind his teeth behind pursed lips. As the anger grew, he threw Junath against the floor, and then said, "If you will not begin to read this book and tell me what you already know, then I will let you share that dungeon with your 'beloved' sister."

Defiance was kindled in Junath's heart, but he finally caved in and said, "Fine, give me the book." He started reading in Matthew chapter one. Shorn took his pose on his throne with his leg draped across the arm and supported his head with his hand. He closed his eyes.

29

A Little Sage

"Why don't you read me something more useful! All you are reading is how this Jesus said he was a king but now he's dying? Even his god has forsaken him. Useless! Where is this glorious weapon?" Shorn's frustration was clearly seen on his face.

Junath simply replied, "This isn't the end, this Jesus rises from the dead, listen a little longer."

"Rises from the dead? Likely story…but continue…"

"Jesus, when he had cried again with a loud voice, yielded up the ghost. And, behold, the veil of the temple was rent in twain from the top to the bottom; and the earth did quake, and the rocks rent; And the graves were opened; and many bodies of the saints which slept arose, And came out of the graves after his resurrection, and went into the holy city, and appeared unto many. Now when the centurion, and they that were with him, watching Jesus, saw the earthquake, and those things that were done, they feared greatly, saying, Truly this was the Son of God. And many women were there beholding afar off, which followed Jesus from Galilee, ministering unto him: Among which was Mary Magdalene, and Mary the mother of James and Joses, and the mother of Zebedee's children. When the evening was come, there came a rich man of Arimathaea, named Joseph, who also himself was Jesus' disciple: He went to Pilate, and begged the body of Jesus. Then Pilate commanded the body to be delivered. And when Joseph had taken the body, he wrapped it in a clean linen cloth, and laid it in his own new tomb, which he had hewn out in the rock: and he rolled a great stone to the door of the sepulchre, and departed. And there was Mary Magdalene, and the other Mary, sitting over against the sepulchre. Now the next day, that followed the day of the preparation, the chief priests and Pharisees came together unto Pilate, Saying, Sir, we remember that that deceiver said, while he was yet alive, After three days I will rise again. Command therefore that the sepulchre be made sure until the third day, lest his disciples come by night, and steal him away, and say unto the people, He is risen from the dead: so the last error shall be worse than the first. Pilate said unto them, Ye have soldiers: go your way, make it as sure as ye can."

"This Pilate, sounds like a reasonable governor. The disciples will surely try to steal the body and fake a resurrection. Keep reading."

Junath continued, "So they went, and made the sepulchre sure, sealing the stone, and setting a watch. In the end of the sabbath, as it began to dawn toward the first day of the week, came Mary Magdalene and the other Mary to see the sepulchre. And, behold, there was a great earthquake: for the angel of the Lord descended from heaven, and came and rolled back the stone from the door, and sat upon it. His countenance was like lightning, and his raiment white as snow: And for fear of him the keepers did shake, and became as dead men. And the angel answered and said unto the women, Fear not ye: for I know that ye seek Jesus, which was crucified. He is not here: for he is risen, as he said. Come, see the place where the Lord lay. And go quickly, and tell his disciples that he is risen from the dead; and, behold, he goeth before you into Galilee; there shall ye see him: lo, I have told you. And they departed quickly from the sepulchre with fear and great joy; and did run to bring his disciples word. And as they went to tell his disciples, behold, Jesus met them, saying, All hail. And they came and held him by the feet, and worshipped him. Then said Jesus unto them, Be not afraid: go tell my brethren that they go into Galilee, and there shall they see me. Now when they were going, behold, some of the soldiers came into the city, and showed unto the chief priests all the things that were done. And when they were assembled with the elders, and had taken counsel, they gave large money unto the soldiers, saying, 'Say ye, His disciples came by night, and stole him away while we slept. And if this come to the governor's ears, we will persuade him, and secure you.' So they took the money, and did as they were taught: and this saying is commonly reported among the Jews until this day."

"This is indeed a strange tale you read. Though this book claims to have a weapon, it's clearly a fable."

"But it doesn't read like one of our fables, this story reads like fact. I think you miss the point. This Jesus is conquering not with a sword, but with the forgiveness of all our wrongs."

"Forgiveness. Who can forgive all wrongs?"

"If this Jesus is the sacrifice chosen by this God mentioned here in this book, then perhaps he truly can forgive sins. Later, after this Jesus goes into heaven, I read in what is called the book of Acts of the Apostles, these Jews were convinced they had done wrong by killing this man, but that this God raised him from the dead, and has truly made him the king. The Jews then asked what they could do about it, and then Peter said for them to repent and be baptized for the forgiveness of their sins. It says that 3000 people were baptized and that Jesus added them to his church. Even further, it says that those who knew Jesus the best, refused to stop teaching in his name even though it meant imprisonment, beatings, and in at least one case I have read so far death. I still have more to read, but I must admit, I think there's truly something to this Christ."

"Is that so little sage? Of course, you would, but for now, you are the prisoner. Keep reading, and find me this weapon if it's there."

"I will, but I still think it's a different kind of weapon you will find."

"Just keep reading." Shorn closed his eyes, and took his normal pose on his throne.

"Then the eleven disciples went away into Galilee, into a mountain where Jesus had appointed them. And when they saw him, they worshipped him: but some doubted. And Jesus came and spake unto them, saying, All power is given unto me in heaven and in earth. Go ye therefore, and teach all nations, baptizing them in the name of the Father, and of the Son, and of the Holy Ghost: Teaching them to observe all things whatsoever I have commanded you: and, lo, I am with you always, even unto the end of the world. Amen."

"All power you say. Well, where is he now? This is ridiculous! Be gone from my presence until I call for you again." Shorn signaled for a guard to come and escort Junath back to his quarters.

30

The Weapon

In his room, Junath sat in a corner and looked around. He was certainly grateful that he no longer was in the pit, but he hadn't seen Isabella since that first day in the throne room. Was she safe? Was she free? Junath wished he could have answers to his questions, but they were impossible to find out. Guards watched his room day and night, and the windows were no use for they were sealed shut. So Junath sunk into his corner to read this book that Shorn was so intrigued by. Perhaps he would find an answer that would satisfy his curiosity.

He plopped the book on the floor and buried his face in his hands moaning with annoyance. When he finally looked down at the book, he noticed the book had opened to part of the bible that he had never seen before. He whispered to himself, "Isaiah…what is this book about?" So Junath began to read.

Moments later, with eyes wide open, he rushed to his door and called for the guards.

"Quiet in there."

"I need to speak with Shorn Forte!"

"You only see him when he calls for you, not on your own time."

"Tell him I have found something intriguing in this book."

There was no reply.

"COME ON!" Junath slammed his back against the door and slid down to the floor frustrated, but just when he thought he would have to wait until the next day, he heard footsteps approaching his room. He stood up waiting for the door to open. When it did, a guard stood in the frame and motioned for him to come.

"Lord Forte has agreed to see you."

"Thank you," Junath said.

When Junath entered the throne room, Shorn looked at Junath and said, "This had better be the weapon I've been looking for."

"No, but it is something that is incredible, and I wanted to share it with you."

"You try my patience, but go ahead."

"We have been reading where Jesus died but rose again."

"You are quickly running out of time."

"I found something, look here in this other part of the book, it's a prophecy. And apparently, according to a note on this page, it says that this prophecy was written about 700 years before Jesus was born."

"Go on, read it then."

"Who hath believed our report? and to whom is the arm of the LORD revealed? For he shall grow up before him as a tender plant, and as a root out of a dry ground: he hath no form nor comeliness; and when we shall see him, there is no beauty that we should desire him. He is despised and rejected of men; a man of sorrows, and acquainted with grief: and we hid as it were our faces from him; he was despised, and we esteemed him not. Surely he hath borne our griefs, and carried our sorrows: yet we did esteem him stricken, smitten of God, and afflicted. But he was wounded for our transgressions, he was bruised for our iniquities: the chastisement of our peace was upon him; and with his stripes we are healed. All we like sheep have gone astray; we have turned every one to his own way; and the LORD hath laid on him the iniquity of us all. He was oppressed, and he was afflicted, yet he opened not his mouth: he is brought as a lamb to the slaughter, and as a sheep before her shearers is dumb, so he openeth not his mouth. He was taken from prison and from judgment: and who shall declare his generation? for he was cut off out of the land of the living: for the transgression of my people was he stricken. And he made his grave with the wicked, and with the rich in his death; because he had done no violence, neither was any deceit in his mouth. Yet it pleased the LORD to bruise him; he hath put him to grief: when thou shalt make his soul an offering for sin, he shall see his seed, he shall prolong his days, and the pleasure of the LORD shall prosper in his hand. He shall see of the travail of his soul, and shall be satisfied: by his knowledge shall my righteous servant justify many; for he shall bear their iniquities. Therefore will I divide him a portion with the great, and he shall divide the spoil with the strong; because he hath poured out his soul unto death: and he was numbered with the transgressors; and he bore the sin of many, and made intercession for the transgressors."

"Is this what you desperately wanted to show me? Who do you think I am! Give me the book and be gone from my sight!"

A guard came up behind Junath, grabbed him by the arms, and dragged him back to his room. Junath yelled as he crossed the threshold back down the hall, "You won't find the weapon you're looking for," but Shorn paid him no attention.

***

That night, while sleeping in his bed, his door was opened and Junath bolted awake, jumping to his feet. There in the door and silhouetted by the lights from the hall, was Shorn Forte. Junath prepared himself to fight not knowing what to expect.

Shorn walked up to him and lifted the book before Junath and said, "Do you believe this book to be true?" His tone was quiet.

Junath looked up into his eyes and replied, "I believe I do or I'm getting close."

"Do you think that this Jesus can truly forgive someone of their sins? All of their sins?"

"He said he could."

"What about my sins? I have done some very wicked things."

"If there's someone capable of forgiving everyone's sins, then he's the only one."

Shorn looked down at the book while pacing around the cell for a few moments.

"Shorn?"

Shorn Forte ignored Junath's prompting, but then opening the book to the place Junath referenced in Acts, he ran his fingers over the words at verse 38 and said, "It says to repent and be baptized for the forgiveness of sins. Junath, I'm tired. I'm not sure how or why, but this book has humbled me. I realize the guilt and the blood on my hands. I grew angry when I read again the passage of his trial. How he was innocent. But then...then it hit me, 'How many innocent people have I killed in the name of my revenge?' The weight of my violent reality is a burden heavier than I expected. If He promises peace, then I want it. Junath, I know this will sound strange, but will you baptize me tonight?"

Stunned by what Junath witnessed before him, it took him a moment before he replied saying, "Yes, I will." Then the hardness of Shorn's face waxed away, and he grasped Junath by the shoulders saying, "Then let's waste no time and head to the river."

Junath quickly got dressed and the two were headed down the hallway, then Shorn stopped and said, "Wait, I have something I must do before I bathe. I must go and see Isabella."

31

Morning Light

Isabella restlessly reclined in her bed. Sleep, since her arrival home, was intermittent at best. Grief overwhelmed her as she remembered the father she knew as a child. The father who was warm but protective. The one who would pretend to be horse, but be honorable and distinguished. When she heard her father's footsteps coming down the hallway, she groaned in her spirit, sick with the expectation of another moment with the monster her father had become.

She heard his boots stop outside of her door, Shorn ordered the sentries, "Open the door."

Light poured into her room when one of the guards opened her door. To her surprise, Shorn didn't enter but gently called into the room saying, "Isabella, I desire to see and tell you important news. Please get dressed and knock on this door when you are ready." Shorn then ordered the door shut, and her room was dark again.

"Odd. What does he have up his sleeve?" Isabella sat up and lit a candle and grabbed her dress. She walked up to the door and said, "Well, here goes," and she knocked signaling she was ready.

The door opened and Shorn and Junath walked into the room. When she saw Junath by his side she grew more puzzled and she asked, "What's going on?"

"Sweetheart," he reached out his hand, but again she reeled preparing herself for another strike, but none came. Shorn lowered his hand and continued, "Isabella, I'm sorry for the evil I have caused you. Tonight, something has changed in me, and I have come to realize that I have been a different man since your mother left me for Prince Traben." Isabella's puzzled expression continued as she tried to comprehend what was happening, and still, she couldn't believe what she was hearing or seeing.

"Isabella, I was wrong, and because of Junath, I see my error, and I aim to correct it. Beginning by being baptized tonight."

Isabella said, "I…I don't understand what is going on. What is this baptized thing you speak of, and what…"

"Listen, I know it's a lot to take in, but please, I want you to come with Junath and me as we go to the river. We'll explain it to you as we go." Shorn grabbed her arm and with a smile said, "Will you come?" Cautiously, she nodded her head, and they were off to the river. Junath summarized the story of Jesus to Isabella as they walked to the river.

By the river, Isabella stood trying to allow this story about Jesus to sink in as she watched her father be dunked under the water and lifted back up. She saw a joy from her father she hadn't seen from him since before her mother left. Then she saw her father baptize Junath and when he came up the two embraced each other as they began a new life devoted to a new king. Seeing their happiness, she knew that this was truly happening.

She came down to the water's edge and said, "Dad, something's truly changed in you. If this Jesus can do it to you, then, I will commit as well.

"Come into the water my daughter," said Shorn. With a large smile on his face, he baptized Isabella in the name of Jesus of Nazareth.

Shorn, Junath, and Isabella went back to the palace. As they entered the palace, he said to his butler, "Danis, I desire to eat now, please bring a plate for the three of us, and..." He looked at his daughter and Junath then he continued, "and have some dry clothes brought down for us."

The trio sat at the table in fresh clothes and the smell of the food was delightful. They started eating, and then Shorn stopped and said, "Jesus gave thanks before he ate, perhaps we should too."

They all agreed and Shorn said, "Lord, we're new at this, but we're grateful that you have chosen us to hear and learn about you. Thank you for everything." Then they ate with gladness in their hearts.

During the meal, Isabella saw her father's face grow stern, and then he said, "At first light, we must be off for I have sent Finister a number of days ago with the orders to begin the attack against Haven. I'm not sure how successful we'll be, but we have to do something."

Junath replied, "Aren't you still the king of Qunereel?"

Reclining back in his chair, Shorn said, "Indeed I am, but my soldiers are quite committed to conquering the world. Finister echoes the sentiment of many in my ranks, and they won't want to lose or forfeit."

Junath said, "I guess we'll have to cross that bridge when we get there, but to delay just gives more time for more to die."

"How true that is, young man."

After the meal, Isabella ran to gather a few things for the trip, and it wasn't long before she rendezvoused with Junath and her father at his flagship. Shorn's personal flagship was similar in size and shape to the other Crimson Airships, but this one was far more ornate with intricate wood carvings and gilded banners. Isabella, going below deck, found a cabin to place her things. Shorn walked in behind her and said, "Daughter, the captain thinks with the current winds, we should only be two and a half days away from the Geor Desert."

"That will cut it close," she said in return. She felt the ship lift, beginning its departure.

"Yes, it's now a race against time. May I give you a hug?"

She looked at her father and said, "There's still a part of me that wants to hold back."

He lowered his head and said, "I know, but I will..." Before he could finish, she embraced him.

"I promise I will do all I can to make it up to you."

"I know, but Jael may not find it as easy to forgive you."

"Well, Junath has, maybe he will too. Besides, I'm waiting for word on something that I think may give me an advantage."

She looked into her father's eyes and said, "What do you have up your sleeve?"

"Patience my dear, I don't want to even get your hopes up."

"Well, when you're ready, then come and let me know. Until then, I'm going to find Junath and see what he's up to."

"I believe I saw him up top at the prow just before I came below."

Isabella gave her father a kiss on his cheek as she left him to find Junath. The Sun was now well over the horizon and scanning the top deck of the ship, Isabella found Junath staring out to the west. Isabella walked up to him and asked, "May I join you?"

Junath said, "Sure."

They sat quietly just enjoying the view when Isabella said, "I want to thank you. I never expected to see my father like this again."

"I'm still in disbelief myself. I was ready for the dungeon when he came into the room. His anger was so deep."

Isabella sighed then said, "It was my mother. My father was a top general in the Qunereel Royal Army, and my parents were asked to be guests by the king on a diplomatic trip to Tuckshire. When my father found that my mother and the Crown Prince of Tuckshire were having an affair, my father went into a deep depression. To cure his depression he became cold, cruel, and vindictive."

Junath then said, "Revenge can be so blinding."

"Yes, and sadly, he kept going. When he refused to listen to me or Jael, we decided to leave. Ever since, Jael and I have been the target of his violence. I guess he felt I abandoned him as my mother did"

Walking up behind them, Shorn said, "That was how I felt, but I was wrong. Your mother never loved me, she just wanted the prestige that came with my position, though I was devoted to her. I always knew where her heart was. But you, you loved me with your every fiber. You pleaded with me to stop, but I wouldn't listen. You didn't abandon me. I drove you away." Isabella then hugged her father and he wrapped his arms around her.

Placing his hand on the back of Junath's neck Shorn said to him, "I have some news for you young man."

Junath said, "Yes sir?"

"I haven't had time to tell you, but that night you ran away from Finister, your father didn't die."

Isabella saw Junath's eyes widen at the news and he nearly lost his balance, but catching himself he asked, "My father isn't dead?"

"No, he isn't. After he recovered, I sent him to one of the prison mines. I sent orders for him to join us in Geor. He should be a day or so behind us."

Junath was speechless, and Isabella looked at her father and said, "Thank you."

32
Battle

Jael stood at the table in the command tent looking at a map of the battlefield. Other officers flanking him were moving pieces on the map indicating the battles raging and the positions either losing or winning. The chancellor was at the other end of the table receiving word from one of the couriers.

Jael said with a point of his finger, "We have to bring the secondary line up the rear here in the eastern zone. Perhaps I can lead the remaining cavalry unit as reinforcements."

Chancellor Manaen said, "Jael, I need you to belay that thought. Word has come to me that three airships have landed west of our position, and there's a clear path to our command tent. The leading ship carries Finister Kein's banner."

Jael said, "Understood sir, I'll depart immediately."

"Careful, my friend, I know you are itching to get Finister, but being rash will get you killed."

"I'll do my best, but don't you worry about me."

On his way out of the tent, Chancellor Manaen grabbed Jael by the arm and looked him in the eye saying, "I'm serious, be careful and don't underestimate him."

Jael said nothing and left. Outside of the command tent he jumped on his horse and rode to the cavalry holding position. When he rode up he gave the orders, "Mount up men, we ride west."

In a matter of minutes, the unit was formed and galloping to the location of the airships. The Crimson army had already cut the distance in half from the airships to the command tent and was making their charge. Unsheathing his sword, Jael called out, "Get ready, men!" After a few seconds, he yelled, "Charge!"

The two forces collided in great pandemonium and the battle was fierce.

Swords clashed and men on both sides fell, but the battle still raged on. Being outnumbered two to one, Jael realized that they were holding their own against the Crimson Cavalry, but the Crimsons had the advantage and were beginning to capitalize on their opportunity. One of the Crimson Cavalry began to wave a red and black flag. Jael felt the pit of stomach knot up in despair as he saw that the flag was a command for one of the airships to come and help press the attack. As the ship approached Jael saw archers line the railings, firing a volley of arrows. Jael yelled, "Shields!" But it was too late for many of his soldiers and their horses were impaled and they fell.

As he clashed swords with a soldier, Jael saw another Crimson soldier racing toward him, but Jael knew he would not have time to pivot to get him. As he braced for the thrust of the sword, an arrow pierced the charging soldier causing him to roll off the back of his horse. Jael finished his fight with the soldier he was fighting, and he turned to see where the arrow had come from. Coming up the hill as swiftly as deer were Cal and Iris.

Cal, while running, was able to reload his bow and fire his arrows in quick succession without missing any of his marks. Iris was able to leap up and pull several soldiers out of their saddles. As a riderless horse got near Cal, he ran alongside it and was able to climb into the saddle. Directing the horse toward the heart of the battle, Cal unloaded several more arrows.

Coming up on his last arrow, Cal tied a rope to it and launched it at an archer on the airship. The arrow arched perfectly and crossing the deck of the ship, it hit an unsuspecting archer who fell over the railing and down toward the battle below. Cal held onto the rope and was pulled by the falling archer, and he landed in the center of the ship's deck. Drawing his sword, he fought gallantly with parries, blocks, and attacks.

He then climbed the side of the balloon and began to cut a gouge into the side of the fabric holding the gas chambers. The airship began to sink and still he cut more causing the craft to speed its descent until it splintered into the ground. Cal rolled off the top of the balloon, landing on his feet. Looking at Jael, he said, "I learned that one from your brother."

The rest of the Crimson soldiers were light work and the Haven cavalry gathered themselves to head toward the other two airships, but as they began to head that way, the two airships were already making their way back across the battle line to the Crimson Command Post.

"Come on, let's head back to Chancellor Manaen and see where we are needed," Jael said to his unit.

The remaining cavalry and Cal with Iris running alongside him made their way back to the command tent. Jael dismounted and entered the tent, and Cal entered behind him.

"Chancellor, we were successful, but we suffered heavy losses. Had it not been for the arrival of Cal and Iris, we would have surely been defeated."

"Glad to hear of some success," said the Chancellor, "The surge we received when Thea and Perri arrived has completely dissipated. We're barely holding the eastern flank." Looking down at the map, he began to point, "If the Crimsons begin to press here and here, we will collapse."

Jael looking at the map said, "Chancellor, my unit is still about 30 strong. Let's split the unit into two. I can take fifteen to support this section and send Cal with the other fifteen to fortify the other."

Cal spoke up and said, "I'll be happy to do that, but let me offer another option. Iris and I have the ability of stealth, allow us to flank and come in from behind to decimate the Crimson Command Post. We can be in and out."

The Chancellor thought for a moment before speaking, "Cal, you have a green light, we could use the advantage that it promises."

Jael spoke up, "But it's a risky move, and his abilities could prove useful on this side of the front."

"True, but any more loss…I'll have to call for a retreat and fortify at the Southern Pass, but still, that would just hold them off momentarily. No, if successful, this will give us the best shot of disrupting their organization." Looking at Cal he said, "Cal, make haste, and may luck be in your favor… may it be in our favor."

"Iris and I will leave straight away."

As Cal turned to exit the tent, another courier stormed in nearly out of breath, but he managed to say, "Sirs, you have got to come out and see this."

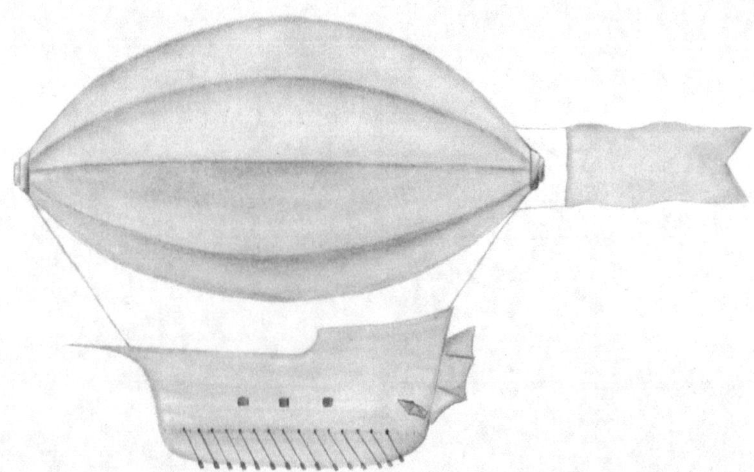

When the Chancellor, Jael, Cal, and the other officers left the tent, they saw Shorn's flagship circling the battlefields with a large white banner. As they passed over the battle zones, the soldiers all stopped their fighting wondering what this could mean. After all soldiers stopped, the airship made a heading toward the Haven Command tent.

The Chancellor said, "Come, let's saddle up and see what this "parley" is all about."

Shorn's flagship landed a few hundred yards from the Haven Command Post and by the time the Chancellor and his party arrived, Shorn, Junath, and Isabella all had stepped off the airship.

33

Peace

Shorn leaned over to Isabella and said, "Go to your husband."

Isabella ran up to Jael and they embraced, but the confusion was obvious on Jael's face and he asked, "What's going on?"

Isabella said, "It's over. He's done with this war, and apparently it's because of your brother."

"Junath?"

"Yeah, that book that he found in the mountains actually worked on my dad, and I guess me too."

Jael said, "I…I don't understand."

"Come, I'll let them explain it to you."

Shorn walked up to the Haven command party, and after being checked for a weapon, reached his hand out to Chancellor Manaen saying, "Chancellor, I offer a truce. I have shed enough blood, let's end it here in peace."

Chancellor Manaen said, "Is this really happening?"

Junath, who had kept silent and behind Shorn Forte, spoke up and said, "Yes your Honor, Shorn Forte is absolutely serious."

The Chancellor took a minute then reached out his hand to grasp Shorn's and said, "Lord Forte, if you desire peace, then peace you have." And looking to Junath he added, "I'm guessing you have quite a story to share if you have a part in this."

Junath said, "Actually, it was this book that convicted him and me both."

Shorn added, "My guilt finally grabbed me by the throat because this book made it living."

Junath said, "Chancellor, This book speaks of a true King who rules and delivers all from their sins. No one is excluded, not even Shorn Forte."

Shorn spoke up saying, "Though I am forgiven of my sins Chancellor Manaen, I must answer to everyone that I have sinned against. Jael, I have been cruel to you, and I should have listened to you and Isabella when you approached me with concern." Then Shorn lowered his head and turned to Cal and said, "With the wolf by your side, I assume you are Cal Whist."

"Aye," Cal's reply was terse and filled with pain.

"Junath has told me what I did to your family. I know an apology will mean little to you because my actions are inexcusable, but I'm truly sorry. What I did against you and so many untold families, I know I can never repay or replace." Cal's face was red with anger, and his eyes welled with tears. Shorn could see that Cal was only growing angrier, so he continued, "Therefore, I surrender my life to Chancellor Manaen. I must answer for my crimes, and if death is the verdict, then it is the least I deserve and I accept it."

Cal said, "Well I can expedite that request."

Cal pulled out a knife with every intention to kill the man before him, but Chancellor Manaen stopped him, saying, "Stand down Cal, Shorn Forte has surrendered to me, and I judge that we hold a joint court with all nations to try him for his war crimes."

Cal said, "I concede but in protest."

"Your protest is duly noted."

"Lord Forte, what is this? You surrender on the eve of your greatest victory?" Everyone turned around and saw Finister Kein red with anger.

"Finister…you don't understand, my greatest victory is peace from my bloodshed. Junath has shown me a new path. A path on which I desire all to follow found within the book he holds."

"You have got to be kidding me! Are you insane?"

With his traditional air of authority, Shorn said, "Finister, it is you who must stand down. I still rule over Qunereel and the Crimson Army. You have no authority here, and it is I who relinquish you of your command."

"You're unfit for command! I will assume the throne and will press this battle. It will be Finister Kein who will be emperor of all Manähu."

"General Kein," Chancellor Manaen spoke up, "I hate to be the bearer of bad news, but at this parley, you are outnumbered."

Shorn then said, "Finister, standdown before they force you to."

Taken aback by Shorn's forceful command, it took a minute for Finister Kein to gather his wits and plan his next move. He finally said, "If that be your wish, then grant me passage to collect my belonging from my tent and the command post."

Shorn looked at Chancellor Manaen, who nodded and said, "Your request is granted."

Finister turned to the officer on his left and whispered something in his ear. The soldier turned and went to prepare the airship for departure. As Finister Kein turned away as if to follow the officer, he grabbed Junath and placed a knife at his throat and yelled, "There will be no armistice, and you, Shorn, have lost all control of the Crimson Army for they answer to me. If anyone comes after me then I will kill this pest of a boy."

Just then, without warning, a flash of white plowed into Finister knocking Junath loose. Lady once again protecting Junath from the clutches of Finister Kein. Finister cried out in pain and reeled back from her, but managed to finally grab her and throw her to the ground. Junath rushed to her side. She was hurt. Before anyone could comprehend what had happened, Finister pulled out his crossbow off his back and aimed an arrow at Shorn.

Jael said, "Put it down Finister, can't you see it's over!"

"Never..." Finister pivoted and aimed the arrow at Chancellor Manaen and fired, but the arrow didn't find its mark for Shorn ran and jumped in front of the Chancellor receiving the fatal arrow instead.

He fell and Isabella ran to his side screaming, "Dad!"

Cal ordered Iris to attack and before Finister could tell where his new adversary was, she had him by the throat pinned to the ground. Chancellor Manaen ordered his officers to arrest him.

Gasping for air, Shorn caressed his daughter's face and said, "I love you." She fell on his chest, sobbing. Then he started calling in a level just above a whisper, "Junath, my boy, come to me."

Junath came and knelt by his side and took his hand. Shorn looked at him and said, "Junath, Thank you for everything and now I am going to put my new faith to the ultimate test…take this word of Jesus to everyone and let them know what He did for me. Me of all people."

Junath said, "I will…I will." He began to sob when Shorn's hand went lifeless. Jael came and comforted both his wife and brother. Shorn Forte, king of Qunereel, and Supreme Commander of the Crimson Army, was dead.

34

Reunion

After the passing of Shorn Forte, all soldiers laid down their arms, packed their gear, and after a couple of days, the camps were all nearly empty. Junath woke early on the third day and looked to the east, awaiting the rising of the sun. Lady lighted next to him and he petted her gently saying, "It's still hard to accept that this is over."

"It is a hard thing." Jael walked up to Junath, handing him a cup of warm coffee and a cornaman. Junath accepted both, peeled the cornaman, and sipped the coffee.

Junath said, "What do we do now?"

"Well, we go home to our families. People rebuild their lives." Then with a nudging of the elbow, Jael continued, "Besides, I think there is a young girl back at Palace Home that was very concerned about a young adventurer off to save his sister-in-law."

Junath began to blush, "Ithleah?"

With a chuckle, Jael said, "You'll just have to get back there and find out."

As the two brothers sat in silence watching the sun crest the horizon, Junath saw a dark silhouette against the morning sky. It was an airship coming from the east. Junath sprang to his feet, and Jael said, "What is it?"

Pointing with his finger he said, "Look, it's an airship. Do you think it could be Dad?"

"I hope so… Oh, I hope so."

After a couple of hours, the brothers saddled their horses and rode out to meet the coming airship. When the airship spotted the two riders it began its descent. Jael and Junath waited eagerly. Then after the ship landed, a worn and tired man stepped to the head of the ramp, and when Junath made eye contact, the man fell onto his knees in tears. Junath jumped off his horse and bounded up the ramp to his father. Jael was right behind him.

Holding his sons tightly, Seren asked, "How is this possible?"

Junath pushed back and looked into his father's eyes and said, "Dad, we're here because of Jesus, who sits on an eternal throne."

"Jesus?"

Junath looked at his father and said, "Dad, I have groaned to see you again. Please come and let me tell you about my adventure."

Junath continued to tell his story and the story of Jesus the Christ not just to his father but to anyone willing to listen. Using the Book of books, Junath continued to declare that by a man named Jesus, we are delivered from the greatest disease and war brought upon mankind. Junath revealed, that the Blood of Christ is the true Crimson Rise.

***

An innocent young troll is ordered to be executed, and it's Charis's fault. Charis, a servant girl, musters her courage to save the young troll. Going against everything she's ever known, Charis must help the troll get back home to her people.

Will they avoid capture?
Will they survive the dangerous forest?
Will the war between the humans and the trolls ever find peace?

www.ingramcontent.com/pod-product-compliance
Lightning Source LLC
Chambersburg PA
CBHW010400310726
48979CB00017B/2799/J

* 9 7 8 1 9 4 8 6 9 6 6 4 7 *